"I think we should talk about last week."

Jeff was right. Before Ariel could say anything, he continued. " I want to apologize for—" He paused.

For what? she wondered. *For kissing me? For making me want you?*

"—letting things get out of hand. I was out of line."

"Apology accepted. We should just concentrate on our business relationship."

"Right. And our...friendship." He smiled, his lips parting slowly, sexily. Ariel couldn't seem to take her eyes off them. "Well," he said. "I guess that's it."

Ariel struggled to control her desire. She put out her hand. Business associates usually shook hands at the end of a meeting.

He took it, and for a breathless, hopeful moment she thought he would pull her into his arms. But that wouldn't do, so she withdrew her hand. "See you."

He nodded and left. As he walked off, he muttered, "Friends? Like *hell*." He knew things were bound to explode sooner or later. Probably sooner...

To my sister, Betty Kurtz, who learned more about hurricanes than she ever wanted to know during Andrew.

And a hug and a kitty treat to Pumpkin, my own weathercat.

Finally, special thanks to Betsy Kaufman and Dr. Neil Frank for answering my questions. I hope I asked enough of them.

THE RELUCTANT HUNK

BY

LORNA MICHAELS

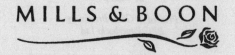

MILLS & BOON

MILLS & BOON and the Rose Device are trademarks of the publisher.
TEMPTATION is a trademark of Harlequin Enterprises II B.V., used
under licence.
First published in Great Britain in 1995
by Harlequin Mills & Boon Limited, Eton House, 18-24 Paradise Road,
Richmond, Surrey TW9 1SR

ISBN 0 263 79495 4

21 - 9511

Printed in Great Britain by
BPC Paperbacks Ltd

Daniel pushed a lock of wavy brown hair off his brow.

"I got a fax from Dad yesterday, so here I am."

Ariel sank into a chair and tried to catch her breath.

"What do you suppose—"

The door to their father's inner office opened. "You may go in now," the secretary announced crisply.

Ariel pulled her blond hair back and tried to appear calm.

1

"CAN'T YOU DRIVE ANY faster?" Ariel Foster leaned forward and shouted at the taxi driver over the din of Led Zeppelin. She looked at her watch—nine-fifty. Only ten minutes left.

"No way, lady. I've already passed my ticket quota for the month." He snapped his gum and blew a bubble as he took a corner. "Got a hot date or somethin'?"

"Or something," Ariel muttered. Actually, she didn't know why she was speeding through Houston, only that she was answering a summons from her father.

"Here we are," the driver said minutes later, as he jerked to a stop in front of KHTX, Houston's Channel 6. "Gee, thanks," he added, as Ariel shoved a bill into his hand and jumped out of the cab.

She spared a couple of seconds to wonder what size bill she'd given him, then shrugged it off. Four minutes left.

In the TV station lobby, she glanced down at her high heels. "To heck with dignity," she decided, yanking them off and running down the hall. When Martin Foster expected you at ten, he didn't mean one minute after.

She thrust open the door of her father's outer office, the momentum carrying her halfway into the room. There she stopped and did a double take. Seated on matching chairs and looking as baffled as she was, were Chad and Daniel, her two older brothers. "You, too?" she said, panting. "Who knows why we're here?"

"Damned if I do," Chad said.

Daniel pushed a lock of wavy brown hair off his brow. "I got a fax from Dad yesterday, so here I am."

Ariel sank into a chair and tried to catch her breath. "What do you suppose—?"

The door to their father's private office opened. "You may go in now," his secretary announced regally.

Ariel patted her blond hair, and tried to appear regal herself as she entered the elegant executive office of the Foster radio-television chain. Still, looking regal wasn't easy when you were five-one in your stocking feet and a hundred pounds soaking wet, but it was worth a try so she did her best to pull it off.

"Hi, Dad." She kissed his cheek, and her brothers shook hands with him, then they took seats around the marble conference table.

Martin Foster smiled. "I called the three of you to Houston to offer you a challenge." His voice boomed through the room.

Ariel kicked Chad under the table and rolled her eyes. They should have guessed. Since childhood, they had participated in dozens, maybe hundreds, of family "challenges." *Okay, Dad*, she thought, *I'm ready. Bring on the next one*.

Chad and Daniel were ready, too. Eagerly leaning forward, they reminded Ariel of horses at the starting gate before a race.

Martin propped an elbow on the table and rubbed his chin. "I've decided thirty-five years of running television stations is long enough. I'm planning to retire next year."

Retire? If Ariel had been wearing socks, her father's words would have knocked them off. Martin Foster—sixty-eight, dynamic, vigorous—retire? The man who'd run a marathon a few months ago, who could still out-arm-wrestle his sons?

Daniel's mouth dropped open. "Why?"

Martin steepled his fingers. "Your mother and I want to spend more time together, travel, enjoy ourselves while we're still young enough."

Ariel looked around the office—thick white carpeting, rosewood desk, a LeRoy Neiman original on the wall. Her father belonged here. He was born for the challenge, the exhilaration of beating out the competition. She couldn't imagine him just lying in the sun somewhere, like a slowly baking potato. *And . . .* "What about the Houston station?" she asked.

"One of you will run it."

Warily, Ariel and her brothers eyed each other. All three had been impatient to move from their smaller markets to more demanding locations. Now they waited for their father's decision.

Martin let the tension build, a half smile on his face. Finally Ariel couldn't stand it any longer. "Who?" she blurted.

Her father grinned. "That's the test. You each have your own station in a competitive market. I'll look at your ratings a year from now. The one who does the best moves to Houston."

In the Foster Entertainment chain, the Houston station was big time. It had the largest audience, the most prestige. Ariel wanted that station; she'd always wanted it.

She pictured herself ensconced behind Martin's massive desk—no, she'd need a smaller one. She imagined chatting with a reporter from *Houston Business Now*. "So, Ms. Foster, how did you go about raising

Channel 6 to new heights?" Heck, why stop with a local publication? Make that a reporter from *Forbes*.

Not only was Channel 6 a prize, but Houston was home. And she'd been away too long.

She glanced once again at her brothers. Chad, the oldest, was practically pawing the ground. Though he looked like a laid-back surfer, with his sun-streaked blond hair and tanned skin, he was a scrapper at heart. Right now he had the light of battle in his dark blue eyes and a smile of consummate confidence on his lips. He was probably mentally packing his bags for Houston.

Daniel was the dark horse; you never knew what to expect of him. He sprawled in his chair and stared out the window behind his father's desk. To a casual observer, he might seem to be gazing at the helipad, studying the logo on the Channel 6 helicopter, but Ariel knew better. Those dreamy brown eyes concealed a razor-sharp intellect. She'd bet that Daniel was already mapping out a ratings-improvement plan for his station.

"So," Martin said, "what do you say? Ready to take me up on the challenge?"

Did he even have to ask? He'd always promoted competition among his children. "Winning isn't everything, but it comes darn close," he'd always said. They were more than ready. And this would be the biggest race of all.

"Sure," Chad replied and winked at Ariel. He sounded as if he'd already won.

"Count me in," Daniel said. "I'm ready to kiss El Paso goodbye."

"Ariel?" Martin asked.

"You bet."

Chad leaned over and patted her shoulder. "Better bow out before the contest starts. You'll never beat me."

Ariel gave him the cockiest grin she could deliver. "Just watch me. I'm going back to Corpus Christi and send my ratings through the roof. A year from now you'll still be living in San Antonio, and I'll be in Houston. I'm going to win."

SHE WAS GOING TO LOSE. The race was almost over. Eight months had passed, and her station was falling behind in the ratings contest. Ariel grimaced at the papers spread on the desk in her Corpus Christi office. She couldn't lose. No, she *wouldn't*.

She got up and paced the room. To her brothers, she described it as compact. Tiny was more like it. Hands on her hips, she glared at the furnishings. Since she'd viewed this placement as temporary, she hadn't bothered redecorating. Everything was standard office fare: fake walnut desk, two black vinyl chairs, a couch covered in tedious tan, and a couple of insipid watercolors on the walls. She was definitely ready for a classy office in a major station. No, more than ready! She strode over to the window and gazed out at her magnificent view of a parking lot.

She drummed her fingers on the pane. She'd paid her dues, working her way up through the Foster chain. Along the way she'd done everything from dusting sets to creating new shows, and done it well. She was as good as her brothers, maybe better. Corpus Christi's Channel 4 had been a good learning experience, but she'd set her heart on Houston. And she was getting desperate.

She flopped down in her chair. As "Our Place in the Sun," the afternoon soap opera, droned on behind her, Ariel rubbed her eyes and checked the ratings again, pondering what she could do to improve them. She'd revamped the morning talk show and the six o'clock evening news, but that hadn't done the trick. If only Channel 12, her local competitor, weren't running the top situation comedy of the year, if only they didn't have a crack news team, if only they hadn't hired that sexy, long-legged female weatherperson. Ariel couldn't do anything about the sitcom, but she needed to beef up the ratings on the news at six. And fast.

Shoving the papers aside, she stared into space as the voices on the television monitor continued.

"Oh, Elliot, it's you I love. I've always loved you."

"Don't take me for a fool, Sabrina. How can I believe you? You're married to Luke, you're carrying Cullen's child—"

"We interrupt this program for a special report from the network."

Ariel spun around and focused on the television monitor.

"The National Weather Service reports that Tropical Storm Belle, moving across the eastern Caribbean, has picked up speed and has been elevated to the status of hurricane. Belle is heading northwest toward the Florida coast at approximately fifteen miles per hour. The hurricane season is three weeks old today. Ten days ago, Hurricane Arthur slammed into the North Carolina coast. Now Belle, a larger and potentially more dangerous storm, is on the move."

Ariel shuddered. Hurricanes! The very thought terrified her. Storms, winds, thunder! "Florida," she muttered to herself. "He said Florida, you ninny. Not Texas. Florida's a thousand miles away."

She let out a breath of relief, then frowned. She'd been so absorbed by her declining ratings, she hadn't given much thought to hurricane season. Last year had been quiet, but this season apparently threatened to be different.

What if a hurricane hit the Texas coast? Did she have the manpower to cover it adequately? Specifically, could her meteorologist, Perry Weston, handle the demands of broadcasting during a major storm? She'd inherited Perry when she'd taken over the station eighteen months ago and hadn't gotten around to replacing him, despite his wooden delivery. She doodled a caricature of him on her notepad—a ventriloquist's dummy, his mouth half open, his trademark bow tie perched beneath a prominent Adam's apple. She'd have to seriously consider doing something about Perry.

"For a projection of hurricane activity this year," the network newscaster continued, "Kent Ackerman is standing by at the National Hurricane Conference meeting in New Orleans. Kent."

"I'm here with Dr. Jeff McBride, formerly of the National Hurricane Center, now with Gulf Coast Weather Technology, a private meteorology firm in Corpus Christi, Texas. Dr. McBride, as an expert on hurricanes, give us your opinion on what appears to be an unusually active summer."

Ariel continued doodling, embellishing Perry's tie with polka dots, adding a paunch drooping over his belt.

"Conditions in the eastern Atlantic are ideal this year for spawning hurricanes—"

Pencil poised in midair, Ariel shut her eyes and listened. Not to what Dr. McBride said, but to *how*. Automatically, she evaluated his voice for its television potential. Deep, resonant. He'd get anyone's attention with that mellow tone and smooth delivery. If he looked as good as he sounded . . .

She raised her eyes to the screen. "Wow!" she whispered. On a scale of one to ten, she gave Dr. McBride an eleven.

He had presence—that elusive, difficult-to-define quality that made people take notice. He looked good. Very good. Strong, masculine features. An appealing trace of five-o'clock-shadow on a tanned face. For a moment, Ariel forgot she was a television executive and viewed him as a woman, appreciating the packaging. "Good Lord, what a waste," she muttered. "He shouldn't be locked away in some science lab. He should be—"

A sharp knock on her door interrupted her fantasy. "Come in," she called, and Steve Loggins, the assistant station manager, charged into the room. Red-haired, freckle-faced, Steve reminded Ariel of a friendly Irish setter. With a smile and a look from those puppy-brown eyes, he could charm the most recalcitrant employee into giving a hundred and ten percent. No one but Ariel knew that behind that affable smile was a man who was painfully shy. But at this moment he was all business.

Nearly out of breath, Steve croaked, "Ariel, there's another hurricane in the Caribbean, and they're predicting major activity this summer. I've been meaning to talk to you, but I've put it off too long." He sank onto the chair opposite her. "We have to do something about Perry."

"Ah, yes. The Man of Wood." She shoved the cartoon she'd sketched across the desk.

"Looks just like him," Steve agreed. "What are we going to do?"

"We could whittle off forty pounds or we could saw him in half. No, wait a minute." She turned back to the monitor, as the network reporter concluded his interview with Dr. McBride.

"Jeff McBride," she muttered. "A meteorologist with a Ph.D., formerly with the National Hurricane Center, now in Corpus Christi." Her voice growing more sure, she continued: "He's right here in town, he's an expert on hurricanes, and he has a face that begs for a camera. Yep, Dr. McBride could solve one of our biggest problems."

Swiveling her chair back toward her desk, she smiled at her assistant. "Get his phone number, Steve. *I want that man.*"

JEFF MCBRIDE WANDERED through the waiting room where Moira Lehrer, the secretary he shared with two other meteorologists, ruled her domain. Preoccupied, he barely noticed her as he passed her desk.

A loud "Ahem" got Jeff's attention and a slip of paper dangling between two long fuchsia-painted nails intruded on his vision. His eyes followed the hand past a wrist surrounded by three gold bangles, up an orange, yellow and lime green sleeve to Moira's face. Good Lord, she'd become a redhead while he was in New Orleans. Or maybe she'd made the change before and he'd been too busy to notice.

"You have a message," she said, gazing pointedly at her hand.

He made no move to take the paper, hoping Moira would handle the call for him. He'd returned from the National Hurricane Conference last night, and he had a mountain of work to catch up on. First on the agenda was the joint project on hurricane tracking he was planning with a professor at Florida State University, which had to be pushed past the professor's uninterested department head. Even a minor interruption now was unwelcome. "What is it?"

"Channel 4," Moira said. "They want to talk to you about doing some spots on hurricanes."

"I did one two days ago."

"That was an interview for the network," Moira told him with exaggerated patience. "This is the local channel, and they must've been impressed because they want you to do some more." She winked at him. "You came across *so-o-o* well on television, they want to make you a star."

Moira grabbed his hand and stuffed the message into it. "Get serious, Moira," Jeff muttered.

"I am, and so was the lady from Channel 4. You should talk to her and see what she has in mind." Her gaze raked over his body. "You'd have every female with a pulse tuning in."

Jeff scowled.

"Okay, okay," Moira said, holding up a hand. "I'm sorry. I forgot you'd rather look like Freddie Krueger than Mel Gibson. But seriously, Jeff, think it over. This community needs educating about hurricanes."

Moira often extended her excellent office-management skills to the lives of the three men she considered her "charges." Though Jeff frequently found this annoying, today he had to admit she was right. He smoothed out the paper he'd started to crumple. "I'll give it some thought and call her back."

He went into his office and shut the door. Despite the papers piled on his desk, he was glad to be back. After the hubbub of the conference, he found the office relaxing. Chairs the deep blue of the Gulf, walls and carpet the tan of the shore, a seascape on one wall, a hurricane chart on another. He never minded the long hours he put in here. He considered his office his sanctuary, the calm eye of a storm.

He glanced at the message Moira had handed him: "Please call about scheduling a series on hurricanes. Ariel Foster, KCOR, Channel 4."

Moira was right about the need for community education. Though they lived in a hurricane-prone area, many people here relied on folk wisdom when a storm threatened. Maybe he could write a column for the Corpus Christi *Mariner*. Yes, he could help people that way. But definitely not on television.

His distrust of the medium was deep-rooted. Several years back, the Tulsa bank where his father was vice president had been involved in an ugly scandal. Television reporters had descended on the family, hounding them unmercifully even though Jeff's father had been clearly innocent of wrongdoing. The publicity had become so ugly that Jeff's fiancée, the daughter of a judge with political aspirations of her own, had called off their engagement. Ever since, Jeff had regarded the news media—television-news gatherers, in particular—as irresponsible sensationalists.

He'd only done the interview in New Orleans because he'd been waylaid. A reporter had thrust a mike in his face as he stepped from the auditorium after presenting a paper at the conference. He'd had no recourse then, but they'd have to hog-tie him and drag him to the TV station before he'd appear on the news on a regular basis.

He remembered one night near the beginning of his doctoral program when a bunch of meteorology students were sitting around, goofing off. Someone had speculated where they'd all be in ten years. They'd appointed one guy head of the National Weather Service, another would be involved in a research project with the Russians. "And McBride will be a TV weatherman," someone had joked.

"Yeah, with his looks, he's a natural."

Even now, Jeff felt the same flush of anger. He hated television, and, even more, he hated being judged by his looks. He'd said nothing but he'd vowed to show his classmates what he really was. And he had. He'd graduated with honors, first in his class. He'd worked hard and achieved success. And he wasn't about to fulfill that prediction of becoming a TV weatherman. Not now. Not ever.

He grabbed the phone and punched in Ariel Foster's number. When he reached her secretary, he didn't bother asking to be put through. "I'd like to leave a message for Ms. Foster," he said. "This is Dr. McBride."

"Yes, sir, Ms. Foster is expecting your call. I'll connect you."

"No, I don't have time to talk. Just tell her I'm not available for television interviews."

He hung up, tossed the message in the trash, and immersed himself in work. When his stomach informed him he'd forgotten to eat lunch, he glanced at his watch. Two o'clock already. He got up, stretched, and left his office, his mind still grappling with the problem of how to squeeze more mileage out of the limited budget promised for the hurricane tracking project.

"Hey, Jeff, watch where you're going." Wayne Nesbit, senior partner at Gulf Coast Weather Technology, adroitly sidestepped him.

"Uh, sorry, Wayne."

Moira looked up from her computer. "Jeff, did you arrange those interviews with Channel 4?"

Wayne halted. "What interviews?"

Jeff tried to make light of Moira's remark. "Nothing important."

He should have known Wayne wouldn't be satisfied with such a vague answer. "What exactly did Channel 4 have in mind?"

"A, uh, series on hurricanes." He edged toward the exit. "I'm not interested."

"Why not?" Wayne asked.

"Personal reasons."

"I'm sorry to hear that. The publicity would be good for you and for the company, too." Though he rarely strayed from his usual mild tone, Wayne always got his message across. And the message now was "Do it."

"Why don't *you* do the series?" Jeff suggested, pleased he'd thought of an alternative. "You're senior partner."

"They didn't ask me."

"I'll call back and recommend you."

Wayne pushed his glasses up on his nose and rubbed a hand over his bald pate. "I'm afraid I'm not television material."

"Neither am I."

Behind him, Moira muttered something under her breath, something that sounded like, "Baloney."

Wayne continued. "South Texas Marine Services will make a decision on the contract we've proposed soon. You know we've got stiff competition. Positive publicity sure could help us."

His boss's quiet words impressed Jeff—but television? The prospect made him shudder. "I'm sorry, Wayne."

"I imagine Florida State would be impressed with a series, too, and maybe What's-his-name, the department head there, would be more supportive of your study. Give it some thought." Wayne headed back to his office.

Jeff waited until his boss was out of earshot, then swung around to face Moira. "Thanks a lot."

She gave him an innocent stare. "For what?"

"'For what?'" he mimicked. "You deliberately mentioned the hurricane series in front of Wayne, didn't you?"

She shrugged. "So what if I did?"

He gritted his teeth. "Moira, I don't—want—to go—on television."

"Horsefeathers," she said airily. "It's your destiny. You're a Sagittarius, aren't you?" She opened her drawer and pulled out the morning edition of the Corpus Christi *Mariner*, then read aloud, "'Sagittarius. A phone call will bring change. Consider all proposals carefully.' See?"

Jeff mumbled an expletive and stalked out of the office. Thanks to Moira, he hadn't heard the last of this. Wayne, in his quiet way, would bring it up again. And he knew Wayne's powers of persuasion. Jeff sighed deeply. He could already feel the rope tightening around his neck.

2

ARIEL PEDALED FURIOUSLY on her stationary bicycle.

She'd received Jeff McBride's message and her temper flared when she read his terse reply. She called him back immediately but got no answer; apparently his office had already closed for the day.

"He didn't even give me a chance to talk to him," she grumbled, brushing the sweat from her brow. "'Not available.'" She pedaled harder. "What a jerk."

Why had he turned her down? Most people would turn cartwheels at the chance to appear on TV. Why not him? He couldn't be nervous; he'd seemed at home in front of the camera the other day.

Maybe he didn't want to be seen because he had a secret past. He was a spy. An embezzler. A bigamist with a posse of wives on his tail. Naw. If that were the case, he'd have avoided the interview in New Orleans, too. Maybe he had some involvement with her competitor. That was it. He was a reclusive billionaire who was the major shareholder in Channel 12. Or maybe he was just too busy. A mundane reason, but more likely to be true.

Her idea had been so perfect, she thought, panting from exertion. The city needed information about hurricanes, the station had an obligation to provide it. And McBride was the one to do it.

Besides, Ariel always trusted her intuition, and her gut feeling told her Jeff McBride would provide the spark her station lacked, and pull viewers back. Half a dozen people had called the station, mentioning his interview. All the callers had been impressed with his knowledge. "And," the switchboard operator had said giggling, "with him." Ariel couldn't let him get away.

What she needed was a plan. The needle on the bike's speedometer edged upward as she considered and discarded one idea after another.

She'd find his home address and camp on his doorstep until he appeared. Nope, too juvenile.

She'd wait for him in the parking lot of his building, throw herself in front of his car. While the idea had a certain flair, she'd probably chicken out at the last minute. Or worse, he might run her over.

No, she decided, slowing her speed, tomorrow morning she'd show up at his office and brazen her way in. She might not make it, but, she recited, "Nothing ventured, nothing gained."

She'd assure him the TV segments wouldn't take too much of his time. She'd guarantee him anything if he'd just consider her offer. But she had to see him first. She slid off the bike. If she succeeded, she'd reward herself with that swimsuit she'd seen in Boutique de la Mer's window last week. And if she failed—

No, forget that. She didn't intend to fail.

She showered and got ready for bed, then repeated her affirmation for the day. "My powers of persuasion are strong. I can convince others of the merit of my ideas." She said it over again twice for luck, then curled up in bed and went to sleep.

The next morning she chose a pale aqua linen suit and gold hoops for her ears. She wore her hair up in a sleek style. She wanted to make an impression, show Dr. McBride how classy, how professional she was. She'd be poised, persuasive, in control. Her arguments would be logical and cogent, appealing to both his mind and his emotions.

She studied herself critically in her full-length mirror, paying particular attention to her shoes. A recent study at the New England Medical Center had revealed that men who were significantly shorter than average were less successful in the workplace. Certain that that applied to women as well, she'd taken to wearing higher heels. She wanted every advantage she could get, especially today with Dr. McBride.

A little feminine allure couldn't hurt, either, she decided, dabbing Shalimar behind each ear. Satisfied, she left her condo, backed her red Corvette out of the garage, and with a roar of the engine, headed for McBride's office.

Since Ariel's secretary had told her he'd returned her call himself, she decided to take a chance that Dr. McBride hadn't shared his decision with *his* secretary and to pretend she had an appointment. She strode confidently into the offices of Gulf Coast Weather Technology.

Seated at the desk in the waiting room was a middle-aged woman wearing a full-sleeved dress in a shocking pink shade that clashed with her bright red hair. Ariel tore her eyes away from the gold feather earrings dangling from the woman's lobes and flashed the secretary a dazzling smile. "I have an appointment with Dr. McBride. I'm Ariel Foster."

"Of course. From Channel 4." The woman seemed delighted she was here. This was going to be a piece of cake. "I watch your morning show every day while I'm getting dressed."

Maybe that accounted for her strange choice of outfits. Too absorbed in the TV. "I'm always glad to meet a viewer, Ms.—" she glanced at the nameplate on the desk "—Lehrer."

On the other hand, Ariel thought, maybe the woman was just weird. Along with the expected, neatly placed secretarial equipment, her desktop contained a paperback copy of *Your Love Signs for the Month* and another entitled *Astrology: Your Guide for Living*.

Ms. Lehrer scanned a brown leather appointment book and frowned. "Are you sure your appointment's today? I don't see your name on the schedule."

Hurdle number one, but Ariel was prepared for that. "We talked late yesterday. He probably didn't write it down."

The woman nodded. "Happens all the time."

"A weatherman with his head in the clouds," Ariel said.

The secretary's eyes twinkled, and Ariel smiled with relief, then noticed Ms. Lehrer glancing at the phone. Ariel fixed her gaze on the woman's hand and concentrated, willing her not to pick up the receiver. *Don't. Please, don't ring his office.*

She didn't. "He must be expecting you," she said pleasantly. "I'll show you in."

Ariel let out a breath. *First hurdle passed. Now for Dr. McBride.*

Ms. Lehrer knocked on a door and opened it halfway. "Jeff, your appointment is here," she said in a how-could-you-have-forgotten-to-tell-me tone.

Before McBride could react, Ariel stepped around the secretary and into the office. Advancing toward his desk, she held out her hand. "Good morning." The door shut behind her. *Good.*

Good Lord, the man was gorgeous. Ten times better looking in person than he was on television. Those gray eyes, that dark, wavy hair that begged a woman to run her fingers through it. She could see a Jeff McBride Fan Club forming.

Now, as he rose from his chair, McBride appeared thoroughly confused. He enveloped her hand with his, stared down at it for a moment, then raised his eyes. "Sit down, please." He gave her a sheepish smile. "Did we have an appointment?"

Ariel took a chair and made herself comfortable. When he was seated, too, she said, "I'm Ariel Foster."

The smile faded. "No, Ms. Foster, we did not." He rose.

Ariel remained seated. "I know."

"Then why are you here?"

"I wanted to talk to you." She gave him her most charming smile.

It didn't work. He scowled at her. "We have nothing to talk about. I thought I made that clear when I called."

If he imagined he could intimidate her, he was wrong. "You didn't listen to my proposition. You can at least do that."

For a moment, their gazes locked in silent combat. Then McBride sat down and checked his watch. "You have five minutes."

A major point won, Ariel smiled. "I can do it in three." She leaned forward. "We've already had two hurricanes this summer. Number three could aim straight for Corpus Christi." He nodded. Encouraged, she continued. "We need to prepare, remind people of the dangers, urge them to take proper precautions. What I have in mind is a series on hurricane preparedness, a short weekly segment—"

"No," he said. "It's a good idea, but I'm busy and I'm not interested. You already have a weather forecaster, don't you?"

In a manner of speaking. "I want an expert on hurricanes," she stressed.

"I'm sure you can find someone else," he said. "I can give you some names—"

Of fat, pot-bellied, boring men like Perry. No, she wanted him. "I'd rather have you."

He put his chin in his hand and stared at her. "Why?"

Because you're sexy. Because just looking into those gray eyes could raise a female viewer's blood pressure, not to mention the station manager's. Because, damn it, I want to win the ratings contest and I need you to help me.

If charm and flattery didn't work, she'd go for guilt. "I'm afraid if we don't educate our residents about hurricane safety, we could have a major disaster. I'd hate to see that happen when the city has an expert like you who could help prevent it." Seeing no alteration in his expression, she decided to be direct. "What can I do to convince you?"

"Nothing. *Nothing* could convince me to go on television."

The force of his words astonished her. "Care to tell me why?"

He stared at her coldly. "I have my reasons."

"Such as?"

He hesitated a moment, then grimaced and said, "Your coverage of Hurricane Clark year before last was oversensationalized. You had people ready to evacuate, caused a traffic jam on the freeway, even a couple of accidents, and then the storm passed us by."

"All the more reason for you to say yes. We need to improve our coverage. With your help, we can." Before he could answer, she added, "I wasn't at Channel 4 two summers ago. I'm here to see that things change."

He gave her a skeptical look. "I told you, I don't have time."

"We'll schedule the segments at your convenience, or we'll tape them in advance, whenever you're free."

"I'm not free."

"But—"

"Sorry, Ms. Foster. You'll have to find someone else."

"But—"

"Look, I'm a scientist. I'm not interested in show business. Television weather reporting."

"That's . . . that's the most ridiculous thing I've ever heard," Ariel sputtered. She knew she was losing her cool, but she couldn't help herself. "TV forecasters aren't actors."

"Aren't they? I remember the Weather Wizard in Tampa. He used to show up every night with a crystal ball."

So that was it. He was afraid she'd ask him to do something embarrassing. "You don't have to worry," she said, in a soothing tone of voice. "I wouldn't ask you to use a crystal ball or do a rain dance. You can be as . . . as scientific as you like."

For a second, she thought she detected a softening of his expression, a slight quirking of the lips, but it disappeared. "I've given you my answer."

She opened her mouth, but before she could get a word out, he glanced at his watch and added, "Your three minutes are up. In fact, your five minutes are up."

She'd been right yesterday. McBride was a jerk. Gorgeous and sexy, but a jerk nevertheless.

Frustrated, Ariel rose and planted her hands on his desk. "Where's your community spirit, Dr. McBride? Corpus Christi needs someone with your expertise. What if a hurricane hits? How will you feel, knowing you could have saved even one life and didn't do it? Think about it." Before he could say any more, before her temper got the best of her, she whirled around and stalked out of his office.

JEFF UNLOCKED THE DOOR of his apartment, glanced at the mail stacked neatly on his coffee table, and ambled into the kitchen, where his once-a-week housekeeper, Opal Hayes, had done her usual thorough job. The stainless-steel stove and the white counter-tops gleamed.

He got himself a beer and, as he twisted off the cap, squinted at the sheet of paper tacked to the refrigerator door with a chili-pepper magnet. Mrs. Hayes, a self-styled expert on feline care, horticulture, and nutrition, frequently left him notes.

Cat is—

"Shelling? Smelling?" He struggled to read the words hidden among the curlicues. "Ah, shedding."

Cat is shedding. Too hot and sunny in here for him. You have to fool him into thinking it's winter. Make it cooler and keep the drapes closed.

"She's imagining things," he muttered, then called, "Blizzard!" A large tomcat padded into the room and rubbed against Jeff's legs, leaving a clump of white fur on his trousers. "You *are* shedding."

Jeff bent to scratch Blizzard's head, then, feeling foolish, turned the thermostat down three degrees and shut the miniblinds over the kitchen window.

Beer in hand, he returned to the living room, kicked off his shoes and leaned back on the couch, propping his feet on the glass-topped coffee table while he read his mail—an invitation to a barbecue at a friend's, a postcard from a woman he dated occasionally who was on vacation, and the usual bills.

Blizzard jumped onto the armchair, leaving more white hair on the navy upholstery. Jeff noticed bits of white on the matching sofa, even on the navy-and-cream dhurie rug. He hoped lowering the temperature would help, or he'd soon have a bald cat on his hands.

He sipped his beer and watched through the full-length window while the sky darkened above the Gulf of Mexico. His thoughts returned to his encounter with Ariel Foster. He'd been taken aback when she'd sailed into his office as if she owned the place. That took nerve. For all she knew, he might very well have scooped her up from the chair and tossed her out on her derriere. To be honest, though, the idea of holding her in his arms was appealing.

He could have done it easily; she was so tiny. Delicate bone structure, small, perfect features—turned-up nose, pouty lips, and eyes the deep turquoise of the Gulf on a sunny day. But no matter how fragile she appeared, the woman had had the audacity to finagle her way into his office, then refuse to leave. She'd leaned across the desk, stared him down and spoken her piece, even in the face of his growing irritation. When he'd turned down her offer, her cheeks had flamed and for just a moment, he'd been sure she wanted to deck him.

He hated to admit it now, but she'd been right. Her last words replayed in his mind. *If you could have saved even one life . . . how will you feel?*

Guilty. He picked up a pillow and heaved it across the room, startling Blizzard and narrowly missing a model ship on the bookcase.

"Damn!" The last thing in the world he wanted was to appear on TV, even temporarily. "Jeff McBride, storm seer," he muttered darkly, imagining himself on a TV set, dressed like a wizard, waving a magic wand at a hurricane tracking chart.

He rarely watched the weather on television, but he'd made a point of checking out both local stations the past two evenings. With her perpetual smile, the woman on Channel 12 looked like an escapee from a toothpaste commercial. Jeff figured she'd keep grinning right through a natural disaster. The guy on Ariel Foster's station—Perry Somebody-or-other—wore garish bow ties and delivered his forecast with the enthusiasm of someone checking for his own name in the obituaries.

Television meteorologists, if they were indeed meteorologists, weren't required to know much about weather other than how to read the National Weather Service's current forecast and turn it into a script. And he was being asked to join that fraternity. That would give his old classmates a laugh, for sure.

But Ariel's words about community needs the other morning had touched a chord. Maybe a family would evacuate in time because of him. Maybe a teenager would stay inside during a storm instead of seeking a dangerous thrill by going surfing. *If you could save even one life . . .*

As if sensing his tension and knowing he needed companionship, Blizzard leaped into Jeff's lap and nuzzled his head against Jeff's jaw. He stroked the cat and stared out the window. The sun had set and now a star winked from the slate blue sky.

What should he do? He wasn't a public person; in fact, he detested the spotlight. But the interview in New Orleans the other day hadn't caused a ripple in his quiet life. Surely a few TV spots wouldn't interfere with his privacy. And they might help Gulf Coast Weather Technology snag the lucrative contract they were vying for. Besides, there was Florida State to consider. Jeff wanted that project to go through. It was a long shot, but perhaps TV appearances would help.

He weighed the pros and cons one more time. The pros won.

Okay, he would do it.

Before he could change his mind, he looked up Channel 4's number, called and asked to leave a message for Ariel Foster. When the operator told him Ms. Foster was still at the station, he wasn't surprised, even though it was almost nine o'clock. She'd struck him as a dynamo.

"Hello," she said. Her voice was soft, throaty... sexy.

"This is Jeff McBride."

She was silent for a moment, then said in a cautious tone, "Well, Dr. McBride. I didn't expect to hear from you. Had a change of heart?"

"Yes."

"You'll do the series for us?" He heard her excitement and imagined those soft lips curving into a smile.

"You convinced me. I'll make the time."

"Wonderful. I'll have a contract drawn up, fax it to you tomorrow, and then we can discuss any changes. Shall I come by your office?"

"Channel 4 is on my way home. Why don't I stop in after work, say around six, one evening this week?"

"How about tomorrow?"

"You work fast, Ms. Foster."

"She who hesitates is lost. That's my motto."

She'd proved that in his office. "I'll see you tomorrow," he said.

ARIEL PUT DOWN THE receiver and restrained herself from giving a whoop of triumph. No longer was he a jerk. Dr. McBride was now a gorgeous, sexy addition to the KCOR staff. She paged Steve and told him the good news, then, noticing that it was nearly nine, went home.

In her bedroom, the message light on her answering machine caught her attention. She pushed the button and listened to her brother Chad's exultant voice. "My ratings are up three points this month. How about yours?"

Ariel scowled at Chad's picture on her nightstand. Since she considered him her most formidable competitor in the race for Houston, she kept his photograph in plain view. She'd halfway considered having it blown up and made into a target, but here beside her bed, it was the first thing she saw in the morning and the last thing at night. That way, she couldn't forget whom she had to beat.

Maybe she'd talk McBride into taking over as full-time weatherman, then she'd wrap up Perry and courier him to Chad. That would undermine Big Brother's ratings.

She replayed his message, picked up the phone to call him, then changed her mind. She didn't want to listen to him gloat. Instead she scribbled a note and faxed it to him: "You know darn well my ratings are down, but I've just begun to fight. Got a new weatherman, and the temperature's about to go up. So don't count your chickens before they hatch, dear. We still have four months to go."

Minutes later her machine transmitted Chad's hand-written reply: "Counting on a weatherman to raise your ratings? Don't you know you shouldn't put all your eggs in one—" he'd crossed out several words and written "—omelet?"

Ariel dashed off an answer: "How do you know he's my only omelet?" Of course, at the moment he was, but Chad didn't need to know that. Then she added, "No reply necessary," and turned off her fax. Let Chad stew all night about her other "omelets."

She went into the kitchen and toasted her successful day with a glass of skim milk. First thing tomorrow, she decided, she'd have McBride's contract drawn up. Second thing was to go straight to Boutique de la Mer and buy that bikini.

3

"COME IN, DR. MCBRIDE." Jeff turned at the sound of Ariel Foster's voice.

She stood framed in the doorway to her office. Her hair, worn loose today, flowed smoothly to her nape, framing her face in a cloud of gold. An image flashed through his mind: sliding his fingers through that golden mane; burying his face in it. He forced the fantasy away and walked toward her. A whiff of perfume—a musky, sexy scent—reached his nostrils.

She put out her hand. He took it and felt petal-soft skin and a firm handshake. Reluctantly, he dropped her hand and followed her into the room, sat and faced her across the desk.

His contract had arrived by fax at quarter past ten this morning. That meant she'd either had her lawyer up all night preparing it or she'd dragged the fellow out of bed at dawn, so she'd been up since then herself. Yet she looked as fresh as if she'd just stepped out of a dressing room. Not a wrinkle showed in her sea blue suit. Energy vibrated from her.

He knew he appeared just the opposite. After a long, tiring day his once-crisp white shirt had wilted, and a hand to his cheek revealed scratchy stubble.

He surveyed her office while she got a copy of his con-tract. Dull, uninteresting. He'd expected more colorful surroundings, given Ariel's personality.

She removed her copy of the papers from a manila folder. Her blue eyes scrutinized him before she spoke. "Any questions about the contract?"

"One or two," he said and watched her pick up a pen with slender, rose-tipped fingers. "In fact, one major disagreement. You asked me to do a weekly segment on hurricanes." He tapped the sheaf of papers in front of him. "What is this about in-depth coverage during a storm? You didn't mention that before."

"No, I added that because I thought you'd want it."

Thought he'd want it? He sat back in the uncomfortable chair and glowered at her. "What gave you that idea?"

She smiled, a slow curving of the lips that threatened to distract him from his annoyance. "By doing the hurricane-preparedness segments, you'll become someone people can trust, someone they depend on. Right?"

"Yes," he agreed grudgingly, certain she was leading him into a corner.

"Then wouldn't you be the person they'd want to turn to if a storm hit? Wouldn't you feel obligated to help them through it?"

She'd cornered him neatly. He wasn't anxious to expand his TV career, but damm it, her argument made sense. "I suppose so."

She lowered her eyes, probably to disguise a gleam of triumph. "Let's hope we don't need additional coverage," she said, "but we may want you for other weather-related spots later on."

He raised a brow. "What kind of weather? Avalanches? Ice storms?"

"Floods." She moved forward and rested her chin on her hand, drawing his attention to the curve of her cheek, the delicacy of her fingers.

Oh, no! He wasn't going to get sidetracked just because he sat across from a beautiful woman. "Only if the floods are caused by a hurricane."

"You're an expert on weather—"

He shook his head before she could continue. "Hurricanes are my specialty. I'll do that for you and nothing else." He saw her mouth open and cut her off. "That's it. Period."

"Maybe we could negotiate."

"Non-negotiable. And the day hurricane season ends, the contract terminates."

"How about an occasional segment afterward on how weather affects the economy along the coast?"

Did the woman never give up? "I told you the other day, I'm a scientist, not a television commentator."

"You could become one," she suggested, and gave him another of those slow, seductive smiles.

If she thought he'd be flattered, she was dead wrong. "Not interested," he snapped, then added, "I'm willing to do the hurricane spots as a service to the community, but that's *all*."

"Okay," she said with an exaggerated sigh and made some notes. Then she looked up with the confident grin he'd already begun to expect from her. "Hurricane season lasts six months. Five more to go. That gives me time to change your mind."

"Don't count on it," he said, but he couldn't suppress a chuckle. The word *chutzpah* must have been invented with Ariel Foster in mind. He saw more than nerve there, however. Behind the sassy smile he'd glimpsed a purely feminine charm that made him think of cool satin sheets and hot loving . . .

He cleared his throat. *Back to business, McBride.*

They settled a few minor points to Jeff's satisfaction, then Ariel said, "We'll start the hurricane series in two weeks. That'll give us time to build up community interest." She flipped on her computer and began typing. "We'll mention the series on the news, add a teaser with your photo to the station logo at various times during the day—"

"No!"

She glanced up with a puzzled look. "I beg your pardon?"

"You heard me. No pictures."

"Why not?"

His temper, which was hovering at simmer, escalated to a boil. "This is science, not show biz."

"This is television," she corrected. "What good will your series do if no one watches? We have to get the viewers' attention."

"And I suppose you were thinking of having me show up at Padre Staples Mall and give out autographed pictures?"

"No, I hadn't thought of that." Her eyes sparkled with mischief. "But, since you brought it up, it's not a bad idea."

"Forget it. Mention the hurricane series on the news, add a line to your logo, but forget about the picture."

She nodded, turned back to the computer, typed some more, then asked, "What's your objection to pictures?"

"I want this series handled professionally. I don't want you using me as the hurricane poster-boy. If people are interested in hurricane prevention, they'll tune in. My face won't bring in a single viewer."

Her lips twitched and she looked as if she wanted to say something, but apparently changed her mind. "How about a pre-series interview on the morning talk show?"

He felt as if he'd been hit by a hurricane himself. Hurricane Ariel! "No interview," he said. "No hype, or *no contract*."

She spread her hands. "Okay. We'll do it your way. I'll make the changes you asked for in the contract and have it delivered to you tomorrow. Kara Taylor, the news-show producer, will call you and set up a meeting to plan the series. She has some great ideas, but I'll let her tell you about them." She typed another line, then looked up and gave him that infuriatingly impudent smile. "You're a tough man, Jeff, but I like challenges. I'm looking forward to working with you."

Looking forward? He'd either end up strangling the woman or— He refused to let his mind complete that thought. "I'm sure our association will be…interesting," he muttered. Then, because he couldn't prevent it, he smiled back at her.

Their gazes locked for a long, potent moment. Something hung in the air between them, sparking the same feeling he got when a storm was about to break—tension, anticipation, excitement. "I'll expect Ms. Taylor's call," Jeff finally said. He got up quickly before he could be sucked under again, and hurried from her office.

Ariel's lips curved as she watched him go. His face wouldn't bring in a single viewer? Apparently the man never looked in the mirror. Once the female population of Corpus Christi got an eyeful of Jeff McBride, the weather would be the hottest game in town.

She smiled lazily. He thought their association would be interesting; *she'd* term it exhilarating. She hadn't met a man who intrigued her this much in a long time.

She'd dated high-powered businessmen but found them exhausting. Immersed in her own demanding career, she wanted a change of pace when she left her office. Jeff McBride, a scientist who shunned the spotlight, was surely that. She pictured him living a tranquil life— taking walks along the beach, spending evenings listening to music. Then she put herself in the picture and grinned. Mixing tranquil and lively was bound to stir something up.

She'd dated handsome men, too; some with the breeding habits of rabbits and IQs to match. Many were so taken by their own looks, they expected nothing less than adoration. Clearly, Jeff didn't care a fig for his appearance. That was refreshing.

She wondered what lay behind his handsome face. She'd like to find out. She *would* find out. She scribbled a new affirmation—"Every day I learn something new and interesting about Jeff McBride—"on a slip of paper and put it in her purse.

She printed out the notes she'd made during their meeting, then paged her secretary. "Peg, fax these notes to Gary Billings so he can make the changes in Dr. McBride's contract. Tell him it's urgent. I'd like the final papers back tomorrow."

She was sure her ratings would rise with McBride's presence on the air. And he'd be an asset to both the station and the city. Such a valuable new colleague should be properly welcomed to Channel 4. And Ariel knew just how to do it. Smiling, she turned again to her computer and typed a reminder to herself.

Next she called Steve. "Mission accomplished. McBride will sign the final contract tomorrow."

"Great! Want to celebrate with a pizza?"

Ariel opened her desk drawer and glanced at the bag from Boutique de la Mer. She'd rewarded herself with the swimsuit. Would pizza have her spilling out of it? No, she decided, she could afford the extra calories, provided she pedaled two extra miles on her bike tonight. "Meet you in five minutes."

When she and Steve were settled at Pizza Italiana with a pepperoni pizza sizzling between them, he told her, "McBride was a good idea. I think he's going to be your ticket to Houston." He raised his beer mug in a toast.

Ariel clinked her ice tea glass against it. "And yours to becoming station manager." Of all her staff here, Steve was the only one she'd confided in about the family contest. Their goals were the same. Both wanted to take the next step up the ladder, and if Ariel moved up, so would Steve.

"How are your brothers doing this month?" Steve asked.

"Better than I'd hoped. Daniel's started a new children's show, in English and Spanish. It's gotten a lot of publicity in El Paso and even some national attention. Daniel's the thinker in the family, the innovator. I'm not surprised he's come up with something fantastic."

"And Chad?"

"He tells me he's working on a great idea, but he won't say what. That's just like him, the rat, to keep it under his hat until he's ready to spring it. He used that strategy when he was on the fencing team in college, too," she added, smiling ruefully at the memory. "He'd hold back, bluff until his opponent got overconfident, then move in for the kill."

"Don't worry," Steve said. "You'll come out ahead."

"I hope so." Since her father's challenge, Houston had beckoned her, a tantalizing pot of gold at the end of the rainbow, always just out of reach. Houston meant home, constancy.

She'd lived a nomad's life too long, moving from station to station in the Foster chain. The one love affair that had mattered to her had ended because of her career demands. She wanted... *needed* a place to settle. And what better place than Houston, the one permanent home she'd known? A sudden feeling of desperation gripped her. What if she didn't win?

Firmly, she pushed the question and the anxiety aside and focused on business. "Know what Kara suggested? That we have McBride follow a family through hurricane awareness, preparation, and if we have to, through an actual storm."

"Good idea. This series is a sure hit."

Trust Steve to boost her morale. Since she'd been here, he'd become her best friend, a surrogate brother without the competitive edge. He'd proved an excellent sounding board for her ideas on how to run a television station, and, in turn, Ariel had provided a sympathetic ear as he'd confided his unrequited passion for Kara Taylor. Unfortunately for Steve, Kara had an unending line of eager admirers vying for her attention.

Now Steve set down his slice of pizza and stared morosely at his plate. "Kara will probably fall head over heels in love, once she sets eyes on McBride."

Ariel grinned. "Don't worry your li'l ole head about Kara. I'll do my very best to keep Dr. McBride occupied."

THE PEAL OF THE DOORBELL penetrated Jeff's sleep. He got out of bed, pulled on a robe, and plodded barefoot to the door, rubbing his eyes. Who'd drop by unannounced this early on a Saturday morning? He glanced at the clock and realized it was later than he'd thought. Still, he considered sleeping late on Saturday sacred, and he didn't appreciate being disturbed.

He opened the door and blinked at a young man holding an arrangement of colorful summer flowers with a shiny balloon in the center. "You must have the wrong apartment."

The youth frowned at the card. "Jeff McBride. Suite 1204."

"That's me, but wh—"

"Sign here, please." He thrust a clipboard and pen into Jeff's hands.

Jeff scrawled his name, took the flowers, and stared, bemused, at the Mylar sun grinning at him from the middle of the bouquet. He put the arrangement on his coffee table, and Blizzard immediately jumped up to investigate, sniffing a yellow daisy, then batting the petals of a zinnia. "Bad cat!" Jeff shook his finger at Blizzard and reached for the card.

Welcome to Channel 4. Please join us for our Fourth of July celebration at the Driftwood Country Club.

Ariel Foster

Even without her signature, he would have identified Ariel's flowing script. After all, he'd seen it on the contract. And in any case, he'd have recognized her style.

Shaking his head, he began to laugh. What a character Ariel was—bold, mischievous, and too darned appealing for his own good. Something had ignited between them the other evening, heating the air, heating *him*. He'd considered exploring that attraction, then listed a dozen reasons why he shouldn't.

They were starting a professional relationship. Did he want to muddy the waters by making it personal? He'd gotten involved with a young meteorologist just starting out when he'd worked at the National Hurricane

Center in Florida, and it had been a disaster. Kay had relied too much on him, expected him to mentor her. When he'd realized she wasn't very competent, both their work and private relationships had turned as blustery as a Category 2 storm. This situation was different, but still . . .

If they got involved, Ariel would badger him to do more broadcasts—and undoubtedly wear him down until he agreed.

She was probably already seeing someone. She was too spirited, too attractive to be alone.

Besides, she was totally different from most of the women he went out with. He liked quiet, intelligent women who enjoyed an evening at the symphony or a peaceful afternoon beachcombing. He could see Ariel was intelligent, but quiet? Never.

His thoughts returned to the picnic. When he'd met Kara Taylor, the news-show producer, she, too, had suggested he drop by on the Fourth. "You'll have a chance to meet the newsroom crew and the rest of the staff," she'd said.

Jeff had thanked her but said he didn't think he could make it. He'd agreed to do the series out of his sense of civic duty; he hadn't agreed to party with the Channel 4 staff. Besides, he'd made tentative plans to go sailing with friends on the Fourth.

Drat Ariel Foster! After a welcome like this, he'd feel like a clod if he didn't show up at the picnic. He shooed Blizzard off the coffee table and gave the flowers a baleful look before he headed for the kitchen. He'd think this through better with a shot of caffeine under his belt.

Rather than wait for fresh coffee, he settled for reheating what was left from yesterday. Blizzard rubbed against his leg, and Jeff glanced down at him. "You're not shedding anymore," he remarked in surprise. "Mrs. Hayes was right, as usual."

Clearly uninterested in the condition of his coat, Blizzard leaped onto the counter while Jeff fumbled in the cabinet for a mug. "Me-ow," the cat demanded.

"Okay." Jeff filled the cat's bowl, and Blizzard dived in.

Jeff poured his coffee and tasted. Strong and bitter. Its kick wiped away the last fogginess of sleep.

He should call Ariel, thank her for the flowers and explain that he couldn't make the party. And she'd probably cajole, argue, exhort—accuse him of rudeness, call him a snob, or worse, threaten a high-powered publicity campaign for his series—until he'd have to give in to shut her up.

All right, he decided, he'd stop by the Driftwood Country Club for an hour, meet the Channel 4 staff, and thank Ariel for the flowers in person. He'd perform his social obligations and still keep Ariel Foster at a distance. After all, what could happen in an hour?

4

ARIEL LOUNGED IN A deck chair beside the pool, enjoying the play of sun on the water, the flags flying in the light afternoon breeze. Her staff and guests were celebrating this Independence Day with exuberance. Cheers from the kids' relay races could be heard across the country-club lawn. A noisy group of adults in the pool periodically drowned out her conversation with Kara Taylor and Heidi Lockhart.

Heidi, columnist for the Corpus Christi *Mariner*'s lifestyle section, was a guest today. Ariel had met Heidi soon after she'd moved to Corpus, and the two had immediately become fast friends. Ariel admired Heidi for her irreverent views on just about everything, and Heidi enjoyed Ariel's flair for mischief.

Heidi took a sip of her bloody Mary and tossed back a lock of long, raven hair. "What do women want?" she asked.

"Just what men want—success, power, satisfaction," Ariel said, lazily applying sun block to her arms. She wore the new bikini, a skimpy little number in turquoise, green and purple.

"Uh-huh," Heidi said. "And what do they want in a man?"

"Now there's an interesting question," Kara said, surveying her bright red toenails.

"If anyone knows the answer, you do," Ariel informed her producer. Kara's admirers were legion, and who could blame them? Not only was she cute and lively, with honey blond hair and a turned-up nose, but she was genuinely nice.

"If I knew for sure, I'd have settled down," Kara said. "Here I am, twenty-nine and still single."

"Not for lack of chances," Ariel reminded.

"We're all single, all pushing thirty," Heidi said with an exaggerated sigh. "So what do we want?"

"Depends what you mean," Ariel replied. "What we're attracted to at first and what we want long-term may not jibe."

"Yeah," Kara said. "And ain't that a shame?"

"Let's start with the outer trappings," Heidi suggested.

"Are we brainstorming one of your columns for 'The Woman's Point of View'?" Ariel asked.

"The first of a two-part series that'll run later in the month. The second focuses on the inner man."

"Is this off-the-record, or are our words gonna come back to haunt us?" Kara wanted to know.

Heidi put her hand over her heart. "I may include your comments, but I won't mention names. You go first, Ariel."

"All right, outer trappings." She considered a moment, then smiled. "I like tall, dark, and brooding. Those hooded eyes get me every time."

A pair of gray eyes sprang to mind. Where was he? The party was two hours old and he hadn't shown up. She felt a surprisingly strong surge of disappointment. After she'd sent him the flowers, she'd considered calling him and asking him to come with her, but then she'd decided that would be overkill. Far better to let *him* make the next move, let him chase her till she caught him. Since he hadn't called, she'd come to the party with Steve, who hadn't mustered the courage to invite Kara. Annoyed at Jeff, Ariel scowled at Heidi. "Why are you writing this? It's so superficial."

"Yeah, it's light reading, but who wants to think when the heat's frying your brain? 'Tis the season to be lazy."

Kara nodded. "So tell us about your summer dream man, Ms. Lockhart."

Heidi's smile was sly. "You'll be surprised, but I'm turned on by a slightly receding hairline and deep-set blue eyes." When Ariel and Kara hooted, she said, "I interviewed the CEO of Lone Star Oil Exploration a few weeks ago. That air of power, mixed with intelligence, turns me on."

Kara shook her head. "Personally, I'll take a blond beach boy. On the other hand," she said, glancing toward the door of the clubhouse and waving, "there's something to be said for tall, dark, and brooding."

Heidi followed Kara's gaze. "I'll say. Who *is* that? If he's one of the lifeguards, I may fall into the pool."

"He's our Monday-night news feature," Kara replied. "He's doing a series on hurricanes."

Hurricanes. Ariel swung around in her chair.

He stood just outside the clubhouse door, surveying the crowd. His white swim trunks contrasted starkly with a tanned, muscular body, and his light blue shirt was unbuttoned to reveal a chest covered with dark, curly hair. Her mouth went dry. The man was a work of art. A sexy work of art.

As if he'd been searching for her, his gaze locked with hers. Slowly, Ariel rose. Over her shoulder, she said to Heidi, "You should watch his first segment and mention him in your column." Then, as she started toward him, she was only dimly aware of her friends' conversation.

"That weatherman is going to take the city by storm," Kara chuckled.

"I believe it," Heidi said. "But if you have any ideas about him, I'd forget them. Looks like someone else has first dibs."

JEFF WATCHED ARIEL approach. Blond hair pulled back in a ponytail, slim legs, golden skin—an abundance of golden skin. He swallowed. An hour with Ariel Foster, and anything could happen. Maybe dropping by wasn't such a good idea, after all. She smiled, and then he was sure it wasn't a good idea.

Her smile broadened when she reached him. "I'm glad you could make it."

"Thank you. And thanks for the flowers. They were a surprise."

Her eyes sparkled. "I like surprising people. Come on." She took his arm. "I'll introduce you to the gang."

She led him first to a middle-age man seated alone, nursing a drink. "This is Perry Weston, our senior weather forecaster."

Jeff recognized Weston. Of course, on TV the weatherman always wore a well-cut suit. In person, with a paunch spilling over his flowered swim trunks and a Texas Rangers baseball cap clamped onto his head, he looked different... and decidedly unfriendly. He offered a stiff hello and a limp handshake.

"Jeff, I'm sure Perry would be happy to give you some tips on television reporting," Ariel added.

"I'd appreciate anything you could tell me," Jeff said, aware that through no fault of his own, he'd invaded Weston's territory and Ariel was trying to smooth the man's ruffled feathers. "As a novice, I could use some help."

"Just be yourself," Perry said, and Ariel's lips quirked.

"Good point," Jeff replied. "Maybe we could get together for a drink sometime and talk."

"I don't drink."

Jeff eyed the glass of whiskey-colored liquid in the man's hand. "Just a conversation then," he suggested, fully expecting Weston to insist he didn't talk, either.

"Maybe," the weatherman muttered.

"Planning to come back after the six o'clock news for the fireworks display, Perry?" Ariel asked, changing the subject. When Weston nodded, she said, "We'll see you later, then," and steered Jeff away.

"Whew!" Jeff murmured. "The wind-chill factor over there was pretty intense."

"I'm afraid Perry sees you as a threat."

Jeff laughed. "I'm not a threat, just a short-term inconvenience."

Ariel smiled but didn't respond. She ushered him from one group to another, rattling off names Jeff was sure he wouldn't remember and job descriptions he didn't understand.

"You have a big crowd here," Jeff observed.

"We have a big station. Some of the folks here are from KCOR Radio, our sister station, and some are guests, but most of them are on my staff."

"Surely the station isn't closed today?"

"Nope. We may doze but we never close. Most of the office staff aren't working, but we still have a skeleton crew on for technical and news. You'll see people coming and going all day." She paused and looked up at him. "Take off your shirt."

"Huh?"

"You're sweating." Her fingertip brushed his chest, where a rivulet slid downward.

She was a natural toucher. As they'd moved from table to table, he'd seen her lay a hand on a shoulder, ruffle a child's hair, but he wondered if she had any idea of the power in her hands. Sweating? That brief contact, fingertip to chest, had set him ablaze. He'd told himself earlier that nothing could happen in an hour. Twenty minutes with Ariel Foster and he felt like he'd been hit by a lightning bolt.

She was still looking at him, and he realized she was waiting for him to remove his shirt. He took it off and slung it over his shoulder.

"That's better," she said. "Now let's get you a drink."

"Great." He needed one, something very cold. They stopped at the bar, then, fortified with a beer, he followed Ariel to a table where two couples sat talking.

She exchanged greetings with the foursome, introduced Jeff, then excused herself. "I need to mingle."

A breather, he thought, relieved, as she walked away. But within minutes, he realized he missed her and found himself glancing around, searching for her in the crowd. When he spied her, she was facing him as if she, too, needed to keep him in sight. Their eyes met, and she sent him a smile clearly designed to dazzle a man. It did.

The group at the table included Kara Taylor, the newsshow producer. With curly blond hair and a ready smile, she looked like the girl you'd take to the senior prom and appeared about the right age, too. But Jeff had learned that her teenage-girl-next-door looks were deceiving. She was sharp and decisive. Her suggestions for his series were good ones. He especially liked the idea of following a family through hurricane season. That would make the series more personal, get people involved.

The others were Steve Loggins, Ariel's assistant manager; Heidi Lockhart, whose byline he'd seen in the

Mariner and Hal Monroe, the evening-news anchor. Jeff considered Monroe a superb anchorman and felt an almost-adolescent pleasure at meeting a television personality in the flesh, then worried if people would start reacting that way to him. *Naw,* he decided. *Not from a few three-minute inserts on the weather.*

As conversation flowed around him, Jeff amused himself by watching his companions. Steve gazed at Kara with mournful, puppy-dog eyes; she seemed unaware of his adoration. Heidi, patriotically attired in a red, white and blue swimsuit, didn't say much but seemed to take in every word.

When Ariel returned, Hal—stocky, fortyish, and possessed of a broadcaster's mellow voice—bemoaned the fact that his wife, a nurse, was on duty today and he, too, had to work most of the holiday weekend.

"Ah, but news never stops," Ariel said. "Besides, you love being where things are happening."

"What's happening here?" Hal scoffed. "We're in the midst of the summer doldrums. My big story last night was a trash bin that caught fire after some kids set off a firecracker."

"Maybe you can come up with a nice, juicy scandal," Ariel suggested, and Jeff felt his stomach clench. Was this how she ran her station, digging up scandals to hype the news? Just the sound of the word brought back memories he'd never been able to put out of his mind. Visions of his father leaving the courthouse after testifying to the grand jury about the bank scandals, his face pale and drawn. Reporters yelling out questions and barring his path. Suddenly the fun went out of the afternoon. He decided to get out of there. Now.

He set his beer down and stood, but a high-pitched scream coming from behind him stopped him cold.

Everyone turned. A small boy, his mouth and chin covered with blood, stumbled toward them. "Daddy!"

Hal jumped from his chair and caught the child in his arms. "Robbie! What happened?"

The youngster didn't answer, just continued crying, and Hal shouted, "Someone get a towel! Get some ice!"

"The lifeguard!" Kara gasped. "He'll have a first-aid kit." She dashed off.

Ariel pressed a napkin to Robbie's mouth as Hal tried to quiet him. Jeff sat down, feeling useless. Nevertheless, this wasn't the time to leave.

A crowd formed, and an older girl pushed forward. "He fell off the swing," she told Hal, who held his sobbing son until the lifeguard rushed over, first-aid kit in hand.

A quick examination revealed Robbie was more frightened than hurt. "He's cut his lip and his chin," the lifeguard said. "I'll clean it with antiseptic and he should be okay."

"No-o-o!" Robbie wailed.

"Robbie, be still," Hal said.

"I'll help you hold him," Ariel offered and put a hand on the child's shoulder. "You're going to be fine," she told him, her voice soft. "The lifeguard's just going to put some medicine on your face."

"Wi-will it h-hurt?" Robbie hiccuped.

"Yes, a little. You'll have to be very brave and very still. Hold my hand, tight." She continued to soothe and reassure Robbie as the lifeguard applied the antiseptic.

"Ooh, it stings," Robbie sobbed.

"I'll blow on it and make it better," Ariel said. Jeff smiled as he watched her blow gently on the cut. He remembered his mother doing that when he was a kid and had come home with a scrape.

The crowd around them dispersed, and Robbie cuddled against his father's shoulder. "You were brave," Ariel told him.

"Like Batman?"

"Yes, exactly like him."

Gingerly, Robbie put a thumb in his mouth. "Do you know any Batman stories?"

She shook her head. "But I do know one about Big Bird and Bert and Ernie. Want to hear it?"

When Robbie nodded, she began. "Once upon a time..."

Of course, Jeff thought, she'd know a story from a TV show. She told it with expression, inserting Robbie himself into the tale, changing her voice to fit the characters, mesmerizing the youngster and Jeff, too.

When the story ended, Robbie wriggled down from his father's lap and trotted off. "He's off to brag about his wounds." Ariel's eyes were soft, her mouth curved in a tender half smile as she watched him head for a group of children. Then she turned to Hal and grinned. "Fatherhood's tough. You look like you need a drink, Dad."

Hal agreed and headed off toward the bar.

Ariel stood and said, "Time to circulate again."

Jeff got up and meandered along with her. They noticed a group of kids playing dodgeball and sat on the grass to watch.

Jeff decided to stay awhile longer. The softer side of Ariel Foster that he'd just seen intrigued him. He wanted to learn more about the woman he'd be working with. Besides, he enjoyed watching her as she laughed and cheered the dodgeball players. "You like kids," he remarked.

"Mmm-hmm. When I was little, I wanted to be a preschool teacher."

He imagined her surrounded by a roomful of toddlers. She'd probably be right down on the floor with them. "Why didn't you?"

She paused for a moment, then shrugged. "When your family's in television, it gets in your blood. You want to be where the action is."

"Do you regret giving up your other dream?" he asked, remembering a few he'd relinquished.

"No. I plan to have children of my own someday," she said. "Meanwhile, I want to have the best TV station in Corpus."

No doubt she would, he thought. He wanted to ask her how she planned to achieve her goal, since he knew her competitor, Channel 12, was currently number one in the city. But someone shouted, "Anyone wanna play volleyball?" and she was on her feet.

"Come on!" She tugged Jeff's arm, and again he decided to stay. They joined a group at the volleyball net and were soon teammates in a rowdy, good-natured game. Ariel played with spirit, spiking the ball, her ponytail bobbing up and down, her voice hoarse from shouting. Jeff enjoyed watching her as much as he enjoyed the game. Spurred on by Ariel, their team routed their opponents. She was a formidable competitor; he'd hate to be on the other side of the net from her—on the other side of anything. He pitied Channel 12.

When the match ended, she mopped her brow. "I need a swim before dinner. How about you?"

Jeff groaned. "Where do you get all that energy?"

"You are what you eat. *I* eat a healthy, balanced diet." She grinned at him and headed for the pool.

She slipped into the water and he slid in beside her. They cooled off, floating lazily side by side. Then Ariel said, "I haven't played volleyball in years, not since college."

"Were you on your college team?"

"No, I just played for fun. I was a fencer."

"Really?"

"Yes," she said, getting out of the pool. Water sluiced down her breasts, and Jeff caught his breath. He imagined stripping away the halter top that covered those sweet mounds, cupping his hands over them, and kissing the nipples to stiffened peaks—and marveled that the water around him hadn't turned to steam.

Ariel sat on the edge of the pool trailing one foot in the water. She was aware of him, too. Her gaze raked over his body with more-than-casual interest. "Fencing's a great sport," she said, continuing the conversation. "It teaches you grace and strategy."

She'd acquired both, Jeff thought, in spades. To conceal his state of arousal, he stayed in the pool but moved to the side where he could tread water and watch her, almost close enough to touch. "I don't know any fencers," he said, resting on his elbows on the edge of the pool and looking up at her. "How'd you get interested?"

"Chad—that's my older brother—was on the fencing team at the University of Texas, and I watched a couple of his matches. I decided if he could do it, so could I."

"So you made the team."

"Yes. I enjoyed myself, but I didn't win as many medals as Chad." She made a face.

Jeff chuckled at her expression. "Someone once said that winning isn't everything."

"And someone else said it's the only thing."

"Is that what you believe, Ariel?" he asked softly.

"I think coming out on top is very important."

"And if you lose?" he murmured.

"I don't think about that." Her expression was solemn now, her voice serious. Jeff wondered why. He wanted to see the sparkle in her eyes again. He ran a finger down her arm, coaxing a smile from her. "I see they're serving dinner on the lawn. Wanna race?"

"No, thanks. Not against those legs of yours. What's the point of a contest I'm sure to lose?"

They feasted on barbecued chicken, potato salad, coleslaw, and watermelon; and Jeff feasted on the sight of Ariel—her golden skin and sparkling eyes. Laughter flowed around them, and he was glad he'd stayed.

Steve, who'd managed to commandeer a seat next to Kara, smiled in obvious contentment. "This is great. Reminds me of big family picnics when I was growing up in Illinois."

Kara smiled at him. "Me, too, except I grew up in Missouri."

"We used to go to Hermann Park in Houston for the big Fourth of July concert," Ariel said. "They'd play the *1812 Overture* and set off cannons, and then there'd be a fireworks display." Again Jeff heard the wistful note in her voice and wondered why it was there. He was wondering a lot about Ariel Foster. The woman had gotten under his skin.

BY THE TIME THEY'D eaten their fill, the sun had set. Ariel smiled to herself. The day had been perfect, and it wasn't over yet.

She and Jeff got up and went to throw away their empty plates. She turned back toward the table, but he said, "Let's take a walk."

She nodded, and they strolled silently, hand in hand, until they reached the children's playground. Ariel stopped beside the swings. She sat on one and pushed off, then smiled at Jeff. "Come on," she urged, and he took the swing beside her.

Ariel lifted her feet, leaned back and let her swing sway back and forth. She remembered loving the dizzy excitement of pumping high when she was a child, but tonight she was satisfied with an easy glide. Her face raised to the sky, she murmured, "There's the first star. We should make a wish." She fixed her eyes on the star, as if staring hard enough could fulfill her desire.

"What did you wish for?" Jeff asked.

She shook her head and pushed higher. "If I tell, it won't come true." She always made the same wish, but whatever star controlled her destiny hadn't granted it yet. She glanced at Jeff as she swung. "What was yours?"

He caught her swing and stopped it. "This."

He stood and stepped in front of her, grasping the chain on either side. Slowly, he pulled her closer. Though her breath seemed frozen, her heart sped up. He leaned toward her, and Ariel's lips parted. His face came closer...closer, and then his mouth touched hers. His tongue traced her lips slowly and sensually; tasting, teasing. He pulled the swing nearer.

And suddenly, without quite knowing how she got there, she was off the swing and in his arms, pressed hard against his chest.

Boom!

They sprang apart.

For a crazy instant, Ariel thought the sound had come from her pounding heart. Then she realized the fireworks had begun. Spirals of red light shattered the darkness and spun haphazardly through the sky. She took a breath and tried to calm herself. Uncertainty, attraction, everything was happening too fast. Like the fireworks gyrating above them, her emotions were spinning out of control. "We should go back," she murmured.

Jeff didn't try to change her mind, but he put his arm around her in a gesture of possession, as if he'd already decided where they were heading but was willing to wait.

They started toward the crowd assembled by the pool. Showers of red, gold and green rose above them. Fireworks hissed and popped, the smell of sulphur and smoke hung in the air. Any other time, Ariel would have been caught up in the spectacle—the cracks and booms as the rockets exploded, the sparks and streaks as they burst into flame and hurtled through the air, the applause of the crowd. But now she could only think of Jeff.

He slowed as they reached a clump of trees. "Let's watch the rest from here." The final barrage of fireworks hit the sky, casting a glow on Jeff's face. He turned to her, put his hands on her shoulders, and drew her toward him. He was going to kiss her again. "Ariel—"

"Ariel," a voice cut in, "do you want to say a few words to the gang before we call it a night?" Steve Loggins stepped out of the shadows.

Startled, she quickly moved out of Jeff's embrace. "S-sure." She turned to Jeff. "I—"

"Go ahead," he said. His voice gave no hint of his feelings.

Reluctantly, she followed Steve but glanced back at Jeff, wishing she could see his face. But the fireworks had died away, and he was cloaked in shadow. What had he started to say?

At the pool, she climbed on a chair and raised her voice. "We've had a great day, with plenty of good food and lots of sunshine. I hope you all enjoyed yourselves with friends and our KCOR family. I know I did."

"You bet," someone said, and applause resounded.

Ariel smiled, then pulled her lips down in a mock grimace. "Now go home and get a good night's sleep. We're back on full schedule tomorrow." That statement was met with good-natured boos.

She hopped down from the chair. "I'll be back in a minute," she said to Steve and headed back the way she had come. But several people waylaid her to say good-night. By the time she broke away and looked for Jeff, he was gone.

5

JEFF STOOD OUTSIDE the small frame house and watched the cameraman set up to tape the family he was to follow through hurricane season. Beside him, Debra Tucker fidgeted and chewed on fingernails that were already gnawed to the quick. "I...I'm not sure this TV thing was such a good idea. What if I say something dumb?"

"You'll do fine," Jeff promised her, then wondered the same thing about himself. He knew the segment was being taped. Still, he couldn't help worrying. What if he flubbed his lines? What if he made an ass of himself—forgot what to do in a hurricane, forgot what city he was in?

"He's right," Kara reassured Debra. "Besides, we can edit out any mistakes, so relax and enjoy yourself. You're going to be a celebrity."

Debra snickered. "Sure. Folks standing behind me in the checkout line at the grocery store will be asking for my autograph. Hear that, kids?" She turned to three youngsters sitting on the porch step, gawking at the camera. "Mama's gonna be a celebrity."

"What's that?" Travis, the oldest, a freckle-faced boy of about seven, asked. Mark and Tammy, the two younger children, listened intently.

"Somebody famous, like Madonna." The kids giggled, and Debra joined in. "Guess they don't see their mom as Madonna. Well, this is as close as I'll ever get." She fluffed her short blond hair and smiled at Jeff.

Her smile was infectious. In some ways, she reminded him of Ariel. Persistent, spunky, and full of life. She'd been one of nearly a hundred to respond to the station's request for a family willing to participate in the hurricane series, and Kara had told him she'd picked Debra immediately, certain the TV audience would identify with the young woman and her children. Jeff had learned Debra was a single mother, trying to get by on meager child support and a job as a clerk in a video store. Life hadn't been easy for her. Still, Debra Tucker kept smiling.

Now, as they waited for the cameraman to give them the go-ahead, Kara signaled the children. "Come on over and stand by your mom. You can be celebrities, too."

As the youngsters gathered around and the cameraman continued checking his equipment, Jeff marveled at the amount of time a three-minute television spot could take.

Earlier in the afternoon, as part of this first segment, he had interviewed several Corpus Christi residents. He'd asked one question: "How do you feel about the prediction that this is going to be an active hurricane season?"

A middle-aged couple, newly relocated from California, had shaken their heads. "We moved here to get away from earthquakes," the husband had groaned, "and now you're talking hurricanes."

An elderly man had scoffed at the mention of serious storms. "Don't see no reason to worry. I've ridden 'em out before." A solemn elementary-school teacher replied she'd instructed her students on hurricane preparedness in science class.

Now they'd zero in on one family, and—

"Ready," the cameraman called.

"Oh, Lord," Debra moaned. "I think I'm gonna be sick."

Me, too. Now Jeff knew another reason he hadn't wanted to go on television: nerves.

Nevertheless, he patted Debra's shoulder. "You'll be great, Madonna. Here we go." He turned toward the camera. "I'm here with Debra Tucker and her family, Corpus Christi residents for a year. But last summer was hurricane-free. How ready are you for a hurricane this year, Mrs. Tucker?"

"I'm not ready at all," she said. "We moved here from Amarillo, and they sure don't have any hurricanes there. I don't know what me and the kids would do if a storm comes. We're pretty close to the beach, here...."

As her voice trailed off, Jeff picked up. "Hurricane awareness and preparation. A necessary part of Gulf Coast life. We'll be following Debra Tucker and her family this summer as she—and you—learn how to protect a family from this deadliest of storms." He completed the rest of his series introduction. The camera stopped and Jeff turned off his mike.

Debra mopped her brow. "Whew! Nerves make you sweat. How'd I do?"

"You were great," Kara said. "You can watch yourself on the six o'clock news."

"Hear that?" Debra said to her kids. "We're gonna be on TV." She turned to Jeff. "Dr. McBride, do you do this a lot?"

"I've done a few interviews, but never a regular series, so today's my first time, too. And the name's Jeff."

"Well, Jeff, you sure make television look easy."

"Easy? You couldn't see what went on inside my head *and* my stomach," he confessed in a whisper.

Debra giggled. "Well, you saved me from fainting or worse, reminding me about Madonna. Thanks." She gestured toward the house. "Would you all like to come in for a drink?"

Kara consulted her watch. "I'm afraid we'll have to take a rain check."

Debra groaned. "Don't mention rain. Makes me think of hurricanes. See you all next week."

They got in the Channel 4 van, and Jeff sighed as the air-conditioning came on. "Debra's right. Nerves make you sweat."

"Come on, McBride, don't tell me a big guy like you gets nervous in front of a little bitty camera," Kara said.

"Damn right, I get nervous. Isn't stage fright one of mankind's universal phobias?"

"I wouldn't know," she said smugly. "I'm never on camera."

Back at the station half an hour later, they started down the corridor toward the news studio and met Ariel coming out of her office. This was the first time Jeff had seen her since July Fourth. She hesitated just long enough for him to see that she was apprehensive about their meeting, but she masked her uneasiness quickly and said, "How'd the afternoon go?"

"Fine." He felt awkward, too, thinking about the other night. The memory of holding her, kissing her, was far too vivid. After Steve had interrupted them, Jeff had watched and listened as she spoke to her staff. He'd seen how wrapped up she was in her work, reminding himself that her career was in television—a medium he thoroughly detested. That thought had the effect of a bucket of cold water thrown in his face. Ariel wasn't a woman to get involved with, even though she fit so well in his arms; even though she'd set off sparks in him that put the fireworks to shame. He'd slipped away, driven to the marina where his friends, Adam and Natalie Gorman, docked their boat, and spent the rest of the evening talking, drinking beer and trying to forget the taste of Ariel's lips.

Now he told himself again he wasn't about to let anything happen between them. He'd make a point of asking What's-her-name out when she returned from her vacation, or he'd call . . . The name of every woman he knew evaporated into thin air, however, to be replaced by one name only: Ariel. He'd told himself the other night that staying out of her way would be simple. *Sure, McBride!* About as simple as pulling back from a magnetic field.

Ariel fell into step beside him and Kara. He tried not to notice the curve of her cheek, the way her blouse hugged her breasts. "You need to change shirts," she said.

Jeff blinked. Was he sweating again? Or did the woman have some sort of shirt fixation? "Why?"

"You've been wearing that shirt all afternoon. You have to look crisp. See if you can dig up another shirt," she told Kara.

"Okay." Kara sized him up. "About a sixteen?"

She'd hit it on the nose, but he didn't want another shirt. "Hey, I'll be wearing a jacket." He held out the suit jacket he'd slung over his arm. "The shirt won't show."

The women ignored him. "Try to find a blue," Ariel said. "It'll blend with his skin tone."

"Okay, and maybe he should shave."

"Mmm, the makeup will—"

"Makeup? What makeup?" Jeff interrupted.

"The makeup that'll keep you from looking pasty on TV," Ariel explained. At his horrified expression, she said, "Walter Cronkite wore makeup. Everyone wears makeup on TV, even Arnold Schwarzenegger."

"Now just a damn minute." Jeff halted in the middle of the corridor. "I'll go along with the makeup, but *I'll* decide if I need a shave. *I'll* decide what shirt I wear." He glared at Ariel. "My contract doesn't give you wardrobe approval."

"Be reasonable, Jeff," Ariel said patiently. "You're going on television. You wouldn't walk into a national meteorology conference looking sloppy."

"I don't look sloppy," he growled, wondering why he'd thought of kissing her again. Throttling her would suit him much better.

"The shirt." Ariel gestured to Kara and the producer jogged off. Ariel turned back to Jeff. "The evening news is important. You have to make an impression."

"Fine, I'll make one." He shoved his arms into his jacket. "See? No spaghetti sauce on my lapel. No holes in my sleeves. Good enough?"

"I suppose it'll have to be." She sighed. "You're an infuriating man."

"And you're a damned irritating woman."

A sudden grin broke over her face. "I guess that makes us even." She put out her hand. "Truce?"

He took it. A mistake. It felt too right. "Truce," he muttered.

"Good. We'll forget the shirt," she called as Kara dashed up, but Jeff swore he heard her add, "This time," under her breath.

He followed Kara. "This makeup stuff is a pain," he complained.

"Goes with the territory, I'm afraid," Kara replied. "It's a fact of life when you're on television and in the public eye."

Community spirit notwithstanding, he didn't want to be in the public eye. Unlike Debra Tucker, he wasn't thrilled by the prospect of becoming a celebrity. So why was he doing this? Because, *if you could save one life . . .* He'd taken Ariel's message to heart.

Jeff met the makeup artist, Lynn Nelson, and sat down, stoically prepared to endure the session. Then he saw the stuff they were about to smear on his face. "Hey, what is this, a Halloween show? I'll look like the Great Pumpkin."

Kara chuckled. "Relax. Under the lights you'll look like a normal human being."

He supposed he'd have to trust her. He watched in the mirror as his face turned neon orange, then followed Kara into the studio.

The six o'clock news was about to begin. Hal, the sports commentator, and Perry Weston—all wearing the same garish makeup as he—were in their positions on the set.

Perry looked up as Jeff came in, glared and said something. Jeff couldn't hear the words, but he could read Perry's lips. Good thing the cameras weren't rolling yet because a comment like that would get the weatherman bumped right off the air.

"You'll be on just before the weather report," Kara whispered. "I'll give you the signal to take your place while we're running the first commercial." She winked at him. "Break a leg, McBride."

ARIEL'S EYES FASTENED on the screen as an exuberant local businessman extolled the merits of his car dealership. Sixty seconds until Jeff's segment.

She'd dreaded seeing him today, unsure how to react. After their torrid kiss at the picnic, he'd just . . . disappeared. What had caused the sudden change of heart? Would they talk about it? Pretend their kiss had never happened? She knew what *she* wanted, but she hadn't a clue how Jeff felt. She'd just have to find out. Maybe after the broadcast . . .

Through the window to the studio, she saw that he'd taken his seat and one of the crew was fastening his microphone to his lapel. Out of sight of the camera, Perry sat glowering at him.

Ariel wondered how Jeff felt. He didn't seem nervous.

"You look nervous, Ariel," Steve said, sliding into the seat beside her.

"How can you tell?"

He snorted. "You're shredding that sheet of paper into a hundred pieces, you're—"

"Okay, so I'm a little antsy." Thirty seconds.

"I don't blame you," Steve said. "I hope McBride doesn't blow it."

"*I* hope he doesn't decide to knock over the desk and walk out. He was mad as heck when I tried to make him change shirts."

Steve choked on a laugh. "I bet he didn't change."

"No, and he didn't shave, either." Ten seconds. She held her breath.

Precisely on cue, Jeff began. "Hurricanes. Nature's mightiest storms . . ."

Ariel let out the breath she'd been holding and settled back, enjoying the sight of his handsome face on the monitor. She made herself forget the way he kissed and concentrated studiously on his camera presence. He was great—superb—and as relaxed and low-key as if he'd done this for years. He'd be the hit of the season. She grinned and gave Steve a high five. "I feel like a mother hen gloating over one of her chicks."

Steve snickered. "Sure you do."

"I discovered him. I feel like he's my chick."

"Right," Steve scoffed. "Remember, I saw you two at the picnic. *Motherly* is the last word I'd use to describe the way you were looking at him."

Ariel felt her face flame. "Umm, why don't we go out for Chinese food after the news?"

"Okay," Steve said. "I guess you want McBride to come along?"

"Sure, and Kara, too."

"You think she'll go?" Steve asked hopefully.

"I'll see to it." When Kara popped into the booth a few minutes later, Ariel extended the invitation and the producer accepted. After the news show, Ariel hurried to catch up with Jeff but saw him heading out with Perry. She supposed they were going to have that talk Jeff had suggested. A good idea, she thought, shrugging off her disappointment.

When they passed the switchboard on their way out, the operator hailed Ariel. "We've had five calls thanking us for the hurricane series."

"Good. Let's run the tape at ten, too," Ariel suggested.

"Sure," Kara agreed. "I can do some shuffling."

They left the building and piled into Steve's car. Ariel sat in the back and watched Steve's ears turn red every time Kara directed a remark to him. Poor guy, he really had it bad.

They indulged in Moo Goo Gai Pan and shop talk, then returned to the station. Kara dashed inside to get ready for the late newscast, and Steve headed home. Ariel followed Kara and made a quick stop at the switchboard. "More calls on the hurricane spot," the operator told her, waving a handful of slips.

"Great." Ariel grabbed them and headed for her office to pick up her briefcase, then left the building, humming to herself as she crossed the parking lot. With calls praising Jeff's series coming in, she was delighted. She'd fax Chad another note when she got home. *Eat your heart out, Big Brother.*

She climbed into her Corvette but noticed something wrong. The car seemed to tilt at an odd angle. "Uh-oh," she muttered and got out. Just as she'd suspected, she had a flat. Darn, she'd been meaning to get new tires, but something always interfered. Now she had no choice. Luckily she had a spare. She opened the trunk, dragged out the spare tire, jack, and lug wrench. From the glove compartment she got a flashlight, then set to work. Within minutes she had the car jacked up and a spot of grease on the front of her new white skirt. "Wonderful," she muttered, gnawing her lip as she concentrated on the unpleasant task.

"What are you doing?"

The deep voice directly behind her made her gasp. "Jeff! You startled me," she cried, but couldn't prevent a surge of pleasure at his presence. Then suddenly the lug nut she'd been struggling with came off and rolled away.

"You *should* be scared. Changing a tire alone in a dark parking lot."

She shrugged at the irritation in his voice and crawled over to see if the lug nut was under her car. Her skirt was already filthy; a bit more dirt wouldn't matter. Over her shoulder, she said, "I'm a big girl. I can handle it."

"Cute," he muttered, his voice ripe with disgust. "Don't you have a security guard here?"

She retrieved the nut and sat back on her heels to look up at him. "Yes, but I don't need help. I can do it myself. I've been changing tires since I was—"

"Knee-high to a grasshopper, I'm sure." He squatted beside her and scowled. "That's not the point. It's dark out here and you're alone."

Ariel responded with a wave of her wrench. "The security guard's a shout away. Besides, there's never been any trouble at the station, and I keep an eye out for anyone who looks suspicious."

"I can't believe you said that," Jeff countered. "*I* just walked up behind you and you didn't notice me until I spoke." He snatched the swinging wrench. "And that's not much of a weapon."

Annoyed, Ariel grabbed for the tool . . . and ended up sprawled half on the pavement and half in his lap, imprisoned by one rock-hard arm.

For a long moment, they both were motionless, staring at one another. Then, ever so slowly, his lips curved and Ariel had trouble breathing. "Let me up," she whispered.

His arm still thrown across her, he shook his head. "You see what can happen in a dark parking lot." His voice thickened, his eyes became two ebony pools.

"Jeff . . ."

Jeff lowered his head. *Just a taste,* he thought, as his lips brushed over her mouth. The wrench in his free hand clattered to the pavement, and his fingers dove into the glorious silk of her hair. She lay in his lap, still and totally pliant, as if she drifted in a sensual haze. Then she twined her arms around his neck, pulled him closer, and kissed him back.

For the second time, he drank in her taste and the sweet, intoxicating fragrance of her body. For the second time, he was aroused by her wild, uninhibited response. He had to stop while he still could. Despite the desperate longing, he lifted his lips from hers.

He picked up the wrench with a hand that shook and helped her to her feet. Her hair was tangled, her lips swollen, her eyes confused. "What—?" she began.

He masked his emotions with logic. "This is a mistake. We're out here where anyone could see us. Do you want to make the ten o'clock news?"

"No." She turned away, but not before he saw the hurt in her eyes.

He put a hand on her shoulder. "Ariel."

"Give me the wrench," she said, in control now, too. "I'll change the tire."

"Jeff—"

"Don't argue," he said, kneeling by the wheel. "Since there's not a cold shower handy, I need to." If he didn't indulge in some physical activity, he'd end up pulling her back into his arms, and they might very well end up on "Headline News."

She nodded and stood behind him, watching while he worked. She said nothing, and he wondered if she felt as flustered as he did. Damn, he'd promised himself he'd keep his distance. That only seemed to work when she was out of sight.

He'd almost finished with the tire when the security guard hurried up to Ariel. "Miz Foster, I saw your flashlight. Everything all right out here?"

"Yes, George. Everything's fine. I had a flat but it's fixed." Jeff heard a tremor in her voice.

"You should've come after me."

"Yes. Yes, I should," she murmured.

"Well, I'll be on my way now, if you're sure...." Ariel nodded and the guard ambled toward the building.

Jeff tightened the last nut, popped the wheel cover back on and lowered the jack. He stood and found himself uncomfortably close to Ariel. His eyes fastened on

her mouth, his heart hammered in his ears. With an ache
as sharp as it was unexpected, he stepped away. "Go
home, Ariel," he muttered. Before she could speak, he
strode across the parking lot.

Dazed, Ariel watched him disappear into the darkness. Hunger and anger warred within her. Once again,
this man had taken her on a crazy roller-coaster ride—
from the heights of desire to the depths of rejection in a
matter of minutes. The other night he'd kissed her and
disappeared; tonight he'd told her flat out that this was
a mistake—and she didn't think he meant just because
they were in the parking lot.

He'd hurt her twice. She wouldn't let him do it again.
She'd keep her distance, think of him only as her ticket
to Houston. From now on, the weather would be decidedly cooler in his vicinity. Icy calm. That was the way to
handle him.

She slammed her car door, drove home at a speed that
would have made a traffic cop cringe, and rode five miles
on her stationary bicycle, visualizing tire tracks on Jeff
McBride's prone body.

6

"AND NOW WE RETURN to today's episode of 'Our Place
in the Sun.'"

Ariel's gaze shifted to the television screen, where two
women faced each other across an elegant living room.

"Luke's not enough for you, is he, Sabrina? Now you
want Elliot back. I've seen the way you look at him, the
way you touch him every chance you get."

"Don't be ridiculous, Angelica. Besides, what do you
care? Elliot's your brother."

"*Step*brother, Sabrina, and don't you forget it."

Ariel turned down the volume. How did Sabrina
manage it? Luke, Elliot, Cullen. Six months pregnant and
she was still a femme fatale. Ariel propped her chin on
her hands and stared morosely into space. Jeff McBride
wouldn't have kissed a woman like *Sabrina* and then
walked away. "Jerk!" she muttered, wadding up a sheet
of paper from her desk and flinging it across the room just
as Kara stepped through the door.

"Direct hit," the producer said with a grin. "Listen,
Ariel, can I send Jeff in to see you when he gets here?
We've discussed some ideas for next week's segment, but
I'd like him to run them by you before we decide."

"Sure, have him stop by. I'll be delighted to see
him—" She waited until Kara had left and closed the
door to add, "And tell him what I think of him." But, of
course, she wouldn't tell him.

So he'd hurt her feelings. She was tough, she could take it. She'd made a mistake—let their relationship get personal. She had to remember that Jeff McBride was a business deal, exactly like "Travelin' Through Texas," a Saturday-afternoon show she'd recently added to improve her ratings. She'd forget about the touch of his lips, the feel of his arms holding her, and she'd be friendly. Business-friendly. Like she was with her seventy-something banker. She'd superimpose the banker's face over Jeff's—wispy gray hair and dentures that clicked when he talked. No problem.

But when Jeff arrived at her office, she found it *was* a problem. Her banker's face didn't fit with the lean, muscular body standing in her doorway. "Kara wanted us to discuss next week's program," he said. His voice was smooth and sexy, without an elderly tremor, without the tiniest denture-click.

Ariel forced a business-associate smile. "Yes, come in."

He took the chair across from her. He wore the same citrusy after-shave he'd had on last week. The scent brought back memories of his cheek pressed against hers. She cleared her throat. "About next week—"

"I think we should talk about last week first."

That was the thing to do. Get the situation out in the open, clear the air. Ariel nodded and took a breath.

"I think we . . ."

"I want to . . ."

"You first," Ariel said. "Go ahead."

"I want to apologize for . . ." He paused.

For what? For kissing me? For making me want you?

"Letting things get out of hand," he continued. "I was out of line."

"Apology accepted," she said briskly, forcing a smile. "We were both out of line. We have a business relationship."

"Right."

A lock of dark hair dipped over his forehead. Her hands itched to brush it back, feel its texture. "So, let's put last week behind us. We're . . . friends."

"Right." His eyes strayed to her mouth.

She watched his pupils widen, saw him shift in his chair. "So, about next week . . ."

He didn't answer. His thoughts seemed to be elsewhere.

"Next week," Ariel prompted.

"Umm, yes. Kara thought of filming Debra and me shopping for supplies. I made a list."

"Good idea. We can do a graphic afterward with the list you have. We'll print checklists and people can send for them, along with hurricane charts." She flipped on her computer, feeling more controlled and businesslike. "We'll put the station logo on the lists and the time of your broadcasts. That'll remind folks to tune in." Pleased with what her station could do for the city, she turned back toward him.

He smiled. His lips parted slowly, sexily. Ariel couldn't seem to get her eyes off them. "Well," he said, half rising, "I guess that's it."

"The, uh, list," Ariel reminded him. She brushed back a tendril of hair from her cheek.

He sat down. "List?" His voice deepened, his gaze riveted on her hand.

"Supply list, so we can do the graphic."

"I have it right here." His hand touched hers as he passed her the paper, and they both started.

"Let's see," Ariel said quickly, trying to hide that flash of sexual awareness. "Batteries, flashlight, candles . . ."

"For when the electricity goes out."

"Electricity," she murmured. There seemed to be no lack of it here. Sparks enough to power the entire station leaped between them. "I'll have the list printed."

"Great." He stood.

She stood.

Ariel walked around her desk. Business associates usually shook hands at the end of a meeting. She put out her hand.

He took it. His grasp tightened. For a breathless moment, Ariel thought he would pull her forward, into his arms. She wanted him to. But Jeff McBride believed in kissing and walking away. She drew her hand back. "See you on TV."

He nodded and left the room. Ariel watched the door shut behind him. "Friends," she muttered. "In a pig's eye, McBride."

Jeff walked off, resisting the impulse to fan himself. Ariel Foster generated more heat than a tropical depression. "Friendship—" he sighed "—like hell." A friendly relationship would only work by long distance. In person, things were bound to explode between them sooner or later. More likely sooner.

ON WEDNESDAY, JEFF arrived at his office late in the afternoon. He'd been at a meeting all day with South Texas Marine Services, and he still had work to catch up on here.

Moira was at her desk, her fingers racing over the computer keyboard. This must be Native American day for her, Jeff decided. She wore a balloon-sleeved, full-skirted dress in aqua and terra-cotta, accented with enough silver to stock half the jewelry stores in Santa Fe—an elaborate Hopi necklace, matching silver-and-turquoise earrings, and an armful of jangling silver bracelets, plus at least half-a-dozen rings. A jewel thief would have a heyday if he didn't collapse under all the weight. Jeff waved at Moira as he passed her, then nodded to two young women from Accounting, who were in the hallway. They looked at each other and giggled.

Jeff shrugged and went into his office. Taking a folder from his briefcase, he spread the contents on his desk. He had a knotty problem to deal with here, and he decided he could do it better with coffee in his system. Grabbing the oversize mug he kept in his office, he headed for the coffeemaker, still pondering the glitch in the software program he hoped to use if the company got the South Texas Marine project. Frowning, he entered the coffee room.

Paul Larson, a fellow meteorologist, came out. "Brooding?" he asked.

"Hmm?"

"You know," Paul said, chuckling. "Brooding, as in 'dark and—'"

Jeff muttered something noncommittal. He *didn't* know, nor did he have time to ask what Paul meant. He poured his coffee and started back to his office. In the hall, he narrowly missed colliding with a college student who was working as a file clerk for the summer. "Excuse me, Dr. McBride," she said, then covered her mouth to stifle a laugh and turned beet red. She scurried into the file room, and Jeff heard whispers and titters as he went by.

Had the entire office suddenly gone crazy? Jeff felt like he'd stepped into the Twilight Zone. Everyone seemed to be laughing, and at him.

He strode into his office and picked up the phone. "Moira, what's going on around here?"

"Wayne's still out of town, the meeting with Mannox Shipping is scheduled for—"

"No, that's not what I mean. Everyone is snickering as if they're in on some private joke, but I don't get it."

"Joke?" Moira paused, then asked, "Have you, um, read the paper today?"

"Just the headlines. I was running late this morning."

"Well, maybe you should. The, uh, life-style section." She sounded uncharacteristically wary. "'The Woman's Point of View.' Want me to bring it to you?"

"Never mind. I have it." He hung up and yanked the paper out of his briefcase, already certain he wasn't going to like what he saw. He flipped to the life-style section and tossed the rest on the floor. "The Woman's Point of View" took up the entire left-hand column of the front page. Heidi Lockhart's face smiled at him from beside the headline, What Do Women Want?

What do we want in a man? No matter what sterling qualities we desire in the inner man, our first glance determines whether we'll look deeper. So, ladies, what turns us on at first sight? Here are seven prototypes of the men we desire.

Jeff grimaced. He'd thought Heidi was too intelligent to write this kind of drivel. He skimmed the column, the types, and, Good Lord, their examples in the community: the Tough, Tanned Cowboy; the Serious, Bespectacled Scholar; Mr. Muscles; then stopped as the next moniker rang a bell: Tall, Dark, and Brooding. "Brooding," Paul had said, "as in dark and—"

Jeff read the paragraph.

Tall, Dark, and Brooding. Lord Byron, Heathcliff. Those intense, haunted eyes under dark brows. Those sensual lips. That cleft in the chin. The look of a poet, a dreamer...or a lover. For the epitome of T, D, and B, catch a glimpse of meteorologist Jeff McBride, who's doing a series on hurricane preparedness on Channel 4 News, Monday nights at six and ten. For devotees of this type, he's not to be missed.

"Goddamn it!" Jeff slammed the paper on the desk. No wonder everyone was laughing. His worst nightmare had come true. And he knew who was responsible.

The telephone rang. "Yes," he growled.

"Dr. McBride, this is Glenda Poe from the Corpus Christi *Mariner*. Since this morning's column, we've had a number of requests to run your picture. Could you send us a glossy?"

"No."

"But—"

"No!" he roared, and slammed down the phone.

That was more than enough. He hated the limelight, he detested having a fuss made over his looks, and he'd had a heaping dose of both. He rolled up the life-style section and charged out of the office. To heck with his briefcase and the folder open on his desk. He wasn't going to get any work done this evening.

"Jeff," Moira ventured, a look of alarm on her face, as he stormed across the waiting room.

"I'm leaving," he snarled. "I won't be back today."

"Oh, dear," she murmured, her hand fluttering to her breast. She grabbed *Your Love Signs for the Month*. Jeff saw her rifling through it as he jerked open the door and slammed it behind him.

He forced himself to obey the speed limit on his way to Channel 4. With his luck, if he didn't, some cop would stop him and write a ticket to Tall, Dark, and Brooding.

He screeched to a stop in the station's parking lot, banged his car door and marched across the lot, ignoring the stares of several people who were leaving the building.

Peg Murphy, Ariel's secretary, looked up as he strode toward her desk. "Hello, Dr. McBr—"

Forget the pleasantries. "Is she in?"

The woman half rose from her chair. "Yes, but she's—"

"Good." He stalked past her and she sank down, a stunned look on her face.

He shoved Ariel's door open and took two steps into the room. She was on the telephone, her chair turned half away from her desk. He let the door slam behind him.

She jolted at the sound and swiveled around. "Let me call you back," she said and hung up. "Jeff," she murmured, "what are you doing here on a Wednesday? Sit down."

As angry as he was, he couldn't help but notice how the late-afternoon sun streaming through the window turned her hair to golden fire, how her lips parted when she saw him. He suppressed those thoughts and slapped the newspaper down on her desk. "Was this your idea?"

He had to give her credit; his harsh tone didn't seem to faze her. She didn't even pretend to misunderstand. "The concept for the column, no," she answered. "Including you in it, yes."

"I *told* you I didn't want any hype."

"You said you didn't want us to use your picture or have you make personal appearances." She tapped the newspaper with her finger and smiled at him triumphantly. "See? No pictures."

He wondered if she knew the *Mariner* had asked for one. "That's beside the point. This makes me sound like—" he forced the words out past throat-tightening anger "—like a sex symbol."

Ariel glanced at the newspaper. "Well, maybe it does. But it's harmless."

"I don't like it," he growled, staring at the offending column.

"Why not? Being mentioned in the column will make you a celebrity."

"I don't want to be a celebrity," he said, frustrated. "At least, not that kind. 'Tall, dark, and brooding,'" he muttered in disgust.

"You are, you know. You're tall, you're dark, and you're brooding right now."

"I'm steaming," he corrected, clenching his jaw.

"Mmm-hmm, but you wouldn't want to be called Tall, Dark, and Steaming, would you?"

Right now, what he wanted was to be a thousand miles away.

"I'm afraid it's too late to burn all of today's copies of the *Mariner*," Ariel continued with an elaborate sigh. "Of course, you could write Heidi and ask her to print a retraction."

"Sure, I can see that now. Heidi'd print the letter, and the whole situation would escalate."

"Quite possibly," Ariel agreed. "Of course, you can say she misunderstood, that you're really short, blond, and—"

"Okay," he said, spreading his hands in defeat. "I get your drift, but I want to be sure you get mine. I don't like this kind of juvenile publicity; I thought I'd made that clear from the beginning. If you have to publicize the series, concentrate on my scientific knowledge." He leaned forward and glared at her. "I'm warning you, if this happens again, I'll consider you in violation of our contract, and I'll be out of here."

Ariel nodded. "I understand. But seriously, Jeff, a lot of people will tune in to see you because of Heidi's article. And they'll learn about hurricane safety in the process."

"I suppose."

"So, why don't you relax and enjoy it? Don't... brood."

He looked up and caught the gleam of mischief in her eyes. In spite of himself, he laughed.

"Truce?" she said, extending her hand.

"For now," he conceded, "provided you agree to my terms."

"All right. Now, the least I can do after all this is buy you dinner. How about it?"

He should say no, leave now and get away from those sparkling eyes and that sassy grin. But he *was* hungry. He might as well accept her invitation. He'd just be careful to keep his mind on alert and his hands to himself. "Sure."

"Give me a few minutes to finish up here."

While he waited, Hal Monroe stuck his head in the door. "Ariel, can I see you for a minute?"

"Sure, come in."

"This is about a possible story, so if I could talk to you in private ..."

Ariel nodded. "Excuse me for a few minutes," she told Jeff.

She shut the door as she left the room, but Hal's deep voice carried. "Remember you told me to find a scandal? Well, I have one."

"Great." Ariel's voice trailed off.

Scandal. Jeff's hands balled into fists. What was he doing, going out to dinner with a woman who worked in a field he despised? Her station was probably like the one in Tulsa, unconcerned about the innocent people whose reputations they ruined. He should get up right now and go home, keep his association with Ariel Foster to a minimum. But her voice echoed in his ears, her perfume lingered in the air. . . .

She opened the door and came into the room, her lips curved in an enchanting smile. "Ready?"

He nodded. *As I'll ever be.*

She took her purse out of a desk drawer and straightened. "Why don't you follow me?"

That was a good idea, he decided. If they rode together, they'd have to return to the parking lot, where there were too many dangerously vivid memories.

SHE TOOK HIM TO Cézanne's, a small French restaurant tucked away on a side street a few blocks from downtown Corpus Christi. Lit by candles, with scenes of Paris on the walls and violin music playing in the background, it was a place for lovers. But Ariel reminded herself that she intended to think of Jeff as a business associate, a casual acquaintance. When their wine came, she raised her glass and said, "To friendship."

"Friendship," Jeff echoed, touching his glass to hers, then murmured, "I've never had a friend quite like you."

She wanted to ask what he meant by that. Instead she said, "'A friend may well be reckoned the masterpiece of Nature.' Ralph Waldo Emerson."

"A literary quotation." He sounded surprised.

"I majored in English."

He gave her a speculative stare and a sexy smile that sent shivers down her back. "I would have expected you to choose something more . . . energetic."

"Like sumo wrestling?"

He chuckled. "Or tap dancing. Besides, English isn't much preparation for running a television station."

Ariel took a sip of wine. "I majored in literature because I love it. I had on-the-job training for station management—I worked at the Houston station every summer."

"Doing what?" His voice husky, he reached across the table and took her hand in his, turned it palm up and traced his thumb over the sensitive skin.

"Everything," she managed, though she seemed to be running out of breath. "My brothers and I were the resident gofers. Of course, we got paid, but Dad worked us like drudges. One summer, though, I had a part on our afternoon children's show."

"What sort of part?"

"The hostess wore a cat costume. I was one of her kittens."

Jeff laughed. "A kitten," he murmured in a voice that said he'd like to stroke her. Then he raised her hand to his lips.

Ariel swallowed. "Jeff." Her voice trembled.

"Hmm?"

"Don't."

His tongue brushed over her palm. Again, shivers danced along her spine. "Why not?"

"We're . . . we're friends."

His lips curved, and he flicked his tongue over her palm again. "Am I being unfriendly?"

"No, but—"

"Chicken Kiev," the waiter's voice interjected.

Jeff dropped her hand, and Ariel scooted it away and buried it, still warm from his kiss, in her lap. Confused, she stared at him as the waiter placed their meals before them. Jeff was trying to seduce her—and succeeding. Why? So he could walk away a third time? She wouldn't allow it. She'd put the evening back on a friendly basis, find a banal topic—the food. "Chicken Kiev's not heart-healthy," she informed him, wrinkling her nose. "Think of all those grams of fat marching into your arteries like enemy soldiers."

His knowing smile told her he was aware she'd deliberately changed the subject. "I'll enjoy the meal anyway," he said, nibbling a flaky buttered roll. "Look, I'm eating my greens," he announced, pointing to the perfectly cooked asparagus.

"In hollandaise," she said, shaking her head and making tsking noises. Jeff laughed and kept eating.

Lest he lead the conversation along more provocative paths, Ariel entertained him during the meal with anecdotes from her childhood—accounts of her tagging along after her brothers, determined to do everything they did. As they talked, she watched him—the glow of candlelight across his face, the crinkles at the corners of his eyes, the way his hands moved. How would they feel on her breasts, her thighs? She wanted to find out— No, she didn't. She didn't know *what* she wanted.

The waiter cleared their plates. *Keep talking. Keep him talking.* "What about you?" she asked. *Are you seeing anyone?* "Umm, how'd you become a meteorologist?"

"Eighth-grade science project. A tornado hit south of Tulsa that year, and I decided to do a study of storm patterns. I took the exhibit to the science fair and won an award from the Meteorology Society—a book on weather—and I was hooked."

"Why'd you specialize in hurricanes?"

"Their power. With all man has accomplished, we're still insignificant compared to the forces of nature. We think we control the world, but we don't. Storms have even shaped history."

"How?" She liked learning more about him and his field.

"Well, the weather played as large a part in defeating the Spanish Armada as the British navy did. The Spanish ships that survived the naval battle tried to escape by sailing around Scotland and Ireland, but a violent gale drove them onto the rocks. Most of the ships never returned to Spain, and her dominance of the seas ended. If they'd avoided the storm, the world might have been completely different."

Enthralled, she leaned her chin on her hand. "That's fascinating. I've always thought meteorology was dull, but it's not, is it? It's science and history. And drama."

"Yes."

"Of course," she said, only half covering a laugh, "maybe Perry has influenced me."

Jeff laughed. "I'm not about to touch that one."

"Jeff," she said suddenly, "what do you think our chances are of getting hit by a hurricane this summer?"

"Fairly good."

Ariel swallowed. Hurricanes that happened several hundred years ago were interesting. The idea of a real one striking Corpus Christi scared her to death. Even a thunderstorm scared her to death. "Will there be much damage?"

"Depends on the strength of the storm. But, with our tracking systems as sophisticated as they are *and* with the hurricane safety series, casualties should be minimal."

Ariel let out a breath as the waiter appeared with the dessert tray.

Jeff declined, but she ordered chocolate cake with raspberry sauce. "Is that part of your heart-healthy diet?" he asked.

She tossed her head. "'The exception proves the rule.' This—" she winked at him "—is the exception."

She ate slowly, savoring every bite. She licked a drop of raspberry sauce from her lips, and his eyes fastened on her tongue. *Uh-oh*, she thought. *Mistake.* "Where have you worked besides Corpus?" she asked quickly.

"Just the National Hurricane Center in Miami. But I decided I wanted more freedom to work on projects that interested me. That's what brought me here."

She shook her head. "Fate."

"Hmm?"

She gestured airily. "You're here, I'm here. Our paths crossed just at the right time—when the city needed your knowledge and I had a way to showcase it. We've formed a good partnership." She wondered if he believed that was all that was between them. *She* certainly didn't.

Soon Ariel asked for the check. The restaurant, which had been full earlier, was now almost deserted. Outside, the breeze that ruffled Jeff's hair brought the scent of the Gulf. "I'll follow you home," he said, "to be sure you get inside safely."

Nothing in his tone or his manner indicated he meant anything more than that. God, the man was confusing, as changeable as the weather. "All right."

When they reached her town house, Ariel leaned out her car window and waved. He waved back and drove away. Ariel went inside, found a large sheet of paper and wrote on it in lipstick, "Jeff McBride—*Business Associate*," then taped it on her bathroom mirror. She should be happy the evening ended as it had; she *was* happy. "Nuts!" she muttered, as she climbed onto her bike and began to pedal.

Jeff headed home, wondering what it would have been like to follow Ariel inside, into her room, to lie beside her, to make love to her through the night. Maybe he should go for it, take her to bed and get her out of his system. *Would* that get her out of his system? He'd never know until he tried, and he'd sure enjoy the effort.

7

JEFF FINISHED THE SPORTS section of the Monday *Mariner* and set it aside. Blizzard immediately appropriated it, stretching out over the baseball scores. Jeff absentmindedly scratched the cat's head and scanned the society column. Then, he groaned, "Oh, hell!" and followed that with a string of expletives so vehement that Blizzard jumped off the table and retreated to the corner behind the refrigerator.

Unbelieving, Jeff read the gossip-column tidbit again. "Sighted at Cézanne's, engaged in intimate conversation, television executive Ariel Foster and—" he could barely stand to read the phrase "—and Hurricane Hunk Jeff McBride." Was Ariel responsible for this, too?

He shut his eyes and dropped his head into his hands. They could have called him a meteorological expert or an atmospheric scientist, but no, they'd said "hunk"! A *hunk* was a guy who sang rock ballads or posed for beefcake pictures, not him! If he had to choose, he'd rather be tall, dark, and brooding.

The telephone rang. Jeff picked it up. "Yeah."

"I didn't do it," Ariel said.

Halfway between a snarl and a laugh, he said, "Be glad, because if you had . . ." He let her imagine the consequences.

"I guess someone phoned it in to the newspaper," she went on. "I apologize."

"You apologize, but you're not sorry."

"Well, it'll attract a bigger audience."

"What kind of audience?" he asked, gnashing his teeth. He seemed to have been doing that a lot since Ariel Foster had stormed into his life; his dentist should send her a commission. "What kind?" he repeated. "Teenage girls, hurricane groupies?"

"Whoever tunes in will learn something," Ariel offered, her voice annoyingly cheerful.

His only comment was a "hmm." Ariel couldn't possibly understand his feelings about publicity, he thought, as he hung up. She'd grown up in a household focused on the media, while his family...

All his parents had asked for was a quiet life. Once, Jeff might have disagreed. When he was younger, he'd been more outgoing and certainly more trusting, but since the banking scandal and the painful breakup of his engagement, he'd seen the value of his parents' goals. The relentless attention of the media had left his father a bitter man and all of them wary of publicity. He hadn't even told his folks he was on television. He hadn't wanted to upset them.

He left his newspaper and coffee cup on the table and drove to the office. "Good morning," Moira sang out when he entered the waiting room. "I'm just thrilled about you and Ms. Foster."

"What about me and Ms. Foster?"

"That you're an item. A *hot* item."

"Moira, we're not an item—"

"Fiddlesticks. Of course, you are." The array of gold circles at her ears tinkled like wind chimes. "She must be a Libra. Find out her birthday for me—exact time and place of birth—and I'll do her chart."

"Moira—"

"Oh, this is so-o-o exciting. Your love was written in the stars. I told you the first time she called that a change was coming."

He leaned over her desk and raised his voice. "Moira! Ms. Foster and I are—*not*—an item. Not a twosome. Not a couple. I'm not 'seeing' her. We're business associates." Of course, only last night he'd been thinking of taking Ariel to bed, but that was none of Moira's business.

Moira nodded sagely and gave him a conspiratorial wink. "I understand." Then she handed him a page from the newspaper. "Here's your daily horoscope. Read it."

He didn't want to read his forecast, but how could he miss it? Moira had highlighted it in shocking pink: "Sagittarius: Expect upheaval today." They could say that again. "Disruptions will continue for the next several days—" *Great!*

From behind him, he heard the sound of feminine laughter and turned to see several secretaries eyeing him and whispering behind their hands. He distinctly heard the word *hunk*. He clapped his hand to his temple. God, he had a headache.

He turned back to Moira. "I'll say it once more, slowly. I am not involved with Ariel Foster. And if I hear any more giggling about that item in today's paper, I'll . . . I'll—" He broke off, at a loss for words. "Just tell them to forget about 'hunk' and concentrate on 'hurricane.' Hurricane Jeff. And remind them hurricanes can be deadly." With that, he stalked into his office and shut the door.

His phone rang. "Hey, pal." It was his sailing buddy, Adam Gorman. "I see you've picked up a new title. What about this Ariel Foster? Is she worthy of a hunk?"

"I'll let you judge for yourself one of these days," Jeff answered, blatantly ignoring the fact that ten minutes earlier he'd told Moira he wasn't seeing Ariel.

The next call was not so pleasant. It came from Tom Carson, vice president of South Texas Marine Services. "I called an hour ago," he began impatiently.

Jeff's watch said three minutes past nine. "Sorry. I just sat down at my desk."

The man harrumphed. "I see your name in the papers every day now. Have you had time to get started on our project or are you too busy hunking around?"

When Jeff assured him he had indeed begun, Carson calmed down, but Jeff's bad mood escalated. Contrary to what Wayne had predicted, he was losing status with his colleagues because of that damn TV series and the resultant publicity. What if word got back to Florida State that he was "hunking around"—whatever that meant? That would be a disaster.

ARIEL THUMBED THROUGH the phone messages and letters on her desk. She opened a bright pink envelope and pulled out a note written in a girlish hand.

Dear Channel 4,
I am a high school sophomore. Last year my science class studied weather, but I wasn't interested. Boy, was I wrong. Hurricanes are megafascinating, especially when Jeff McBride talks about them. Could you ask him to send me an autographed picture, a hurricane chart and a reading list? I want to learn all I can about storms.

Jody Miller

Ariel grinned. No surprise that Jody enjoyed learning

about hurricanes from an instructor who looked like Jeff. Too bad Jeff was so prickly about pictures.

She wrote a reply.

Dear Jody,

Thank you for your letter. We are glad you are enjoying learning about hurricanes from Dr. McBride. Unfortunately, he doesn't have photos available, but here is a hurricane chart with his autograph, and a reading list. Keep watching.

Ariel Foster

She'd ask Jeff to suggest some books for Jody and autograph the chart when he came in this evening.

Thanks to Jeff, their resident hunk, and to Ariel's other recent innovations, Channel 4's audience was growing by leaps and bounds. But Jeff wouldn't be around forever; she needed to secure her improved ratings. Next step was to jazz up her news team. She punched in her father's private number. When he answered, she got right to the point. "Dad, I want to hire a female coanchor for the evening news. Would you spread the word through the chain?"

"I'll send a memo today."

"What's new with Chad and Daniel?"

"Chad's started editorializing on the air," her father answered. "Daniel's doing a six-part anticrime series." Ariel grimaced and began doodling a caricature of each brother. "What about you?" Martin asked.

Ariel smiled. "I've started a weekly three-minute feature on hurricanes. It's generated a lot of interest."

"Hurricanes?" He sounded unimpressed. "That weatherman of yours couldn't generate interest in a national disaster, let alone a nonexistent hurricane."

Ariel drew a skull and crossbones over Chad's face and another over Daniel's. "You haven't seen my hurricane guy. He looks like a movie star." *And he kisses like heaven.*

"What have you done? Hired a male model to read on the air?" Her father's voice was disapproving.

"No, no, Dad. He has credentials, even a Ph.D. He's a combination meteorologist-hunk."

"A *what?*"

"Hunk. The newspapers are calling him the Hurricane Hunk."

"Really?" Martin chuckled. "Make the most of it."

"Oh, I will."

When she hung up, though, she looked back at Jody's letter and sighed. Too bad Jeff was so averse to cashing in on his fame. She could make more of it, if only he'd cooperate.

JEFF PULLED OUT OF THE parking lot and headed toward the grocery store to meet Debra and the Channel 4 crew to tape their shopping trip. He'd immersed himself in work all morning, therefore he was able to get away early this afternoon. With time to spare, he decided to stop by the dry cleaner's to pick up some shirts.

The middle-aged woman behind the counter smiled broadly when he walked in. "Hello."

Jeff nodded. "I have a pickup. McBr—"

"Oh, you don't have to tell me your name," she interrupted, waving her hand. "I know who you are. You're Mr. Hunk."

Jeff didn't answer. What could he say?

While he waited for his shirts, he asked himself how he could have expected life to be normal when he was involved with Ariel Foster and her TV station. Of course, it was his own fault. He'd let her talk him into this insanity. He should have his head examined.

He paid for the shirts and drove to the grocery store. The taping went smoothly. Debra apparently hadn't read the society column because she said nothing about his new title. Perry Weston, however, sneered at him when they ran into one another as Jeff arrived at the TV station to prepare for the live segment. "The sex symbol," he muttered. Jeff ignored the comment, but his anger went up another notch.

He told himself to relax as he settled in for his weekly makeup session. He chatted with Lynn Nelson, the makeup artist, an exotic-looking woman with waist-length black hair, as she worked. She was midway through transforming him into an orange ghoul when a knock sounded on the door. "Come in," she called.

Kara entered the room, followed by Ariel. Jeff focused on Ariel. She'd brushed her hair back and secured it with a gold clip. She wore a pale green skirt and matching blouse in some kind of silky material that swirled around her. Slim gold loops dangled from her ears. Even in a room filled with the odor of cosmetics, he could pick out her delicate scent. Even on a day when he wanted to strangle her, he met her eyes and forgot that there was anyone else in the room.

"Hi," she said in that throaty voice that sounded like it belonged in a bedroom. "I've come to ask a favor."

That put him on the alert. Favors to Ariel could result in catastrophe. "What?"

She held up a stack of papers. "We had a letter today from a high school student. She said you've inspired her to study storms and asked for a reading list and your autograph." She thrust a pen into his hand.

That seemed harmless enough. He signed his name. "I'll put together a reading list and fax it to you tomorrow."

"Thanks." Ariel perched on a stool as Lynn continued working on him. Jeff imagined Ariel in Lynn's place—*Ariel's* fingertips smoothing the makeup over his face, *Ariel* brushing his hair back from his brow, bending closer to kiss him. What was it about the woman that transformed the heat of his anger into flames of desire?

Ariel's brow furrowed as she scrutinized him. "Kara, the tie."

Uh-oh. "What's wrong with my tie?" Jeff muttered.

"Too bland," Ariel said.

"Much too," Kara agreed.

"Mmm-hmm," Lynn added.

Ariel lifted the end of the tie, and the three women examined it, grimacing as if it were a rag he'd bought at a secondhand store.

"This is an expensive tie," Jeff grumbled.

"You can hardly see the pattern," Lynn said, shaking her head.

"It's dull," Kara chimed in.

"Insipid," Ariel said. "This maroon is too dark. Get him one with a brighter red or maybe something with silver."

"Right." Kara scurried out.

"And we should do something with his hair," Ariel continued, oblivious to Jeff's rapidly escalating temper.

"News show's started," came a voice outside the door. "We need you in the studio in five minutes, Dr. McBride."

"Some mousse?" Lynn said, cocking her head. "No, let's put in a wave or two." She reached for the curling iron.

"Like hell," Jeff growled.

Ariel put her hand on his shoulder. "Relax, Jeff. This will only take a minute. You have plenty of time."

Before he could say another word, the curling iron descended on his head, gripping his hair in its heated jaws and closing with a snap. "Ow!"

"Tender headed? Sorry," Lynn said. "I'll be done soon." She released his hair and grasped another strand with the curling iron while he sat helplessly in the chair. "There."

Jeff stared in horror at the two large corkscrews she'd constructed at the crown of his head. Lynn whipped a comb out of her pocket and began monkeying with his hair, pulling it one way, then another until she was satisfied. She stood back. "What do you think?" she asked Ariel.

Why didn't they ask him what *he* thought?

"Nice," Ariel said.

Kara dashed into the room, two ties dangling from her arm. She held them against his chest. "Which one?"

"The one with the red," Ariel decided.

"Yeah. Let's get his off."

Damn it, they were talking about him as if he weren't real, as if he were a puppet they could manipulate any way they liked.

Ariel reached for his tie and began working at the knot.

Lynn was still surveying her handiwork. "Some hair spray, I think," she murmured, and got a can from the counter.

"Okay, that's it!" Jeff roared, bolting out of the chair as Lynn aimed a shower of hair spray in his direction. He jerked off his tie and unbuttoned his collar. "I've had enough." He yanked off his jacket and rolled up his shirtsleeves. "You're treating me like some damn show-biz dummy. Forget it!" he shouted, running his fingers through his newly coiffed hair. "You wanted a scientist, you're getting a damn scientist. *This* is how I work!"

Leaving a roomful of stunned women behind, he headed for the news studio. "That'll show them," he gloated.

KARA GOT HER BREATH first. "Should I go after him?"

"Never mind. It's too late. We'd have an uproar on the set," Ariel said. She turned to Lynn, who stood with her finger glued to the button of the spray can. "You're spraying your shoes."

"Oh!" Lynn stared at her soaked pumps.

"Buy a new pair. The station will pay," Ariel said. "Come on, Kara."

They headed for the control booth and took their seats as Jeff began his segment.

"I can't believe this," Kara whispered. "Look at him. On camera in shirtsleeves."

"Yeah, look at him." Ariel gestured toward the monitor. Though he had recovered his equilibrium and spoke in his usual well-modulated tone, his eyes were still bright with anger. Wisps of dark curly chest hair showed at the vee of his open collar, his rolled-up sleeves revealed tanned forearms, his hair was attractively tousled. He was gorgeous—every woman's dream, hers included, right here on local TV.

Ariel began to laugh, holding her sides and shaking with mirth. "Kara, after tonight's show, there won't be a woman in Corpus who'll miss our Monday-night news. McBride's already made an impression. Now he'll be the toast of the town. He doesn't realize it yet, but he just shot himself in the foot."

8

JEFF SHUT THE DOOR and tossed his briefcase on the couch. After his explosion last night and a busy day today, he wanted nothing more than to relax in front of the tube. Well, maybe not. He'd had more than enough of TV lately. A book would be a better choice—science fiction.

Blizzard met him in the kitchen. The cat paced the countertop, stridently meowing for his dinner. "Okay, buddy, cool it," Jeff ordered. He reached into the cabinet for the bag of cat food. It was empty. Disgusted, he checked the refrigerator for leftovers that could hold Blizzard for a while. Nothing but baloney.

Jeff put a slice of baloney in Blizzard's dish. The cat jumped down, sniffed it warily, and turned away, flicking his tail in disdain.

Jeff scowled at the cat. "Do you have to be so finicky?"

"Meow!"

Usually he bought prescription cat food at the vet's, but this was clearly an emergency. Resigned to his fate, he faced the cat. "All right, fella. I'll go to the store." Blizzard trailed him, meowing imperiously, as Jeff headed for the door.

He drove to the supermarket, hurried inside, and tossed half-a-dozen cans of cat food in a basket. Halfway to the checkout counter, he heard footsteps behind him, then voices.

"It's him."

"Oh, wow! The Hurricane Hunk."

Should he duck down the cereal aisle? Dump the cat food and escape? Too late. Three giggling young women approached him.

A curvy blonde in amazingly short spandex shorts and a T-shirt that revealed as much as it covered batted her eyelashes at him. "We lo-ove your show, Mr. McBride," she gushed.

Her dark-haired companion nodded vigorously. She wore— Lord, he didn't want to guess what it was . . . or wasn't. "We saw you last night. The unbuttoned shirt was *so* sexy."

"Could we have your autograph?" the third, a sandy-haired cheerleader type, asked breathlessly. They crowded around him, cornering him against a detergent display.

"Uh, sure," he mumbled.

"I'll hold your basket," the brunette offered.

"Here's my grocery list," the cheerleader said. As he looked for something to write against, she twirled around. "Use my back."

The giggles continued as he scribbled his name on one grocery list, then another. The blonde pulled a dollar bill from her wallet. "I don't have a list, but you can sign this." She stepped closer and Jeff backed up, dislodging a box of fabric softener. "We go to Texas Tech," she added. "Is there any chance you're coming to Lubbock to lecture in the fall?"

"Not many hurricanes out on the plains," he said, handing her the bill.

"Thank you," they chorused. As he strode away, he heard them chattering in the background.

"Mmm!"

"Isn't he just too cute?"

"Awesome. I'll never spend this dollar."

Face flaming, he slapped some bills on the checkout counter, grabbed his sack and hotfooted it to his car. His outburst last night had backfired. Big time.

ARIEL TRIED TO GAUGE Jeff's mood as he entered her office. A week had passed since his blowup. Surely by now he'd calmed down. His demeanor gave nothing away. "Peg said you wanted to see me," he said, sitting across from her.

"Yes. How'd your week go?"

"Don't ask."

"I...guess you've had some reaction to Monday night's show."

He sighed and shoveled his fingers through his hair. "Encounters at the supermarket, notes in my mailbox, messages on my answering machine. Man, people can be pushy. I'm thinking of getting an unlisted number so I can sleep at night. I got a call at three this morning, offering— Never mind."

"You've gotten some mail here, too." She motioned to the corner, where a large cardboard box overflowing with letters sat.

Jeff stared at it. His mouth worked, but nothing came out.

"Maybe you'd like to read a few," she suggested. "You can use my computer for replies."

"Sure," he mumbled and dragged the box to her desk. She left him shaking his head and muttering something about not believing his eyes.

Ariel hurried to one of the conference rooms where she joined the evening-news team gathered around the table. Kara sat at the head, chairing the meeting. "Stories for this week?" she asked.

A beach cleanup, a petition from a citizens' group requesting more police, and a murder investigation in one of the city's upper-class neighborhoods were mentioned. "What else?" Kara asked.

Hal Monroe stretched out his long legs and tipped his chair back. "I've talked to Ariel about this. I heard a rumor about some dirty dealings going on at St. Elizabeth's Hospital."

"They're expanding, aren't they?" Steve asked.

"Right. They're about to break ground for a new children's wing next door to the main building."

"Yeah," Kara said. "That was a major expansion for them."

"More major than you know," Hal said. "My contact tells me a member of the board has an interest in that next-door property. He has to have made a killing on that sale."

"Uh-oh," Steve said. "Do I smell a rat here?"

"A nasty one," Hal observed. "I need to confirm it with at least one more source before we break it."

"Check it out," Ariel said. She hoped the rumor wasn't true, but if it was, the city needed to know. And the story would be a coup for the station. She imagined her ratings zooming upward, overtaking Chad's and Daniel's. *And in the stretch it's Ariel, coming from behind. Ariel, making her move. Coming up to the finish line, it's Ariel. Ariel wins by a nose!*

When she returned to her office after the meeting, she found Jeff seated at her PC, shirtsleeves rolled up. She stood in the doorway a minute and stared at him. God, even his elbows were sexy. But "sexy" had never been enough for her. "Interesting" was more important, and

Jeff was that. He was also intelligent, a man of principle. And thanks to him, next summer at this time she'd probably be in Houston. A relationship with him would be futile, even assuming he wanted to get involved with her. Judging from the way he kissed and walked off, he didn't. Could she change his mind? Did she want to? Wishing life wasn't so confusing, she walked across the room and leaned over his shoulder to read the letter on the desk beside him.

Dear Dr. McBride,
I am nine years old. Sence I've seen your show, I've desided to be a meater owlajist when I grow up. Could you send me some stuff about kurears?
Sean Wellman

Jeff chuckled, typed a reply, made a note to include career information, and dropped Sean's letter onto one of two piles on the floor beside him. He opened the next letter.

Dear Jeff,
I've waited all my life for someone like you. I am twenty-nine, five-eight, thirty-six twenty-four thirty-eight. My phone number is 555-8319. I sleep in the nude. Do you?
Candy Lowell

"Mmm, Candy. Sweet," Ariel said.
Jeff snorted and tossed the letter onto the larger heap.
"I suppose that's File Thirteen?"
"The lewd and nude one."
Ariel laughed and curled up on the couch to read her own mail.

"Listen to this one," Jeff said.

Dear Dr. McBride,
You and Channel 4 are doing a great service for the citizens of Corpus Christi. I lived through Hurricane Connie in 1983, and I know how important preparation can be. Thank you for your community spirit.

"This one should be addressed to you," he added. "You're the one who made it happen."

"But you carried it through."

"Because you coerced me." His eyes met hers. Something shone there. If she didn't know better, she'd think it was desire. But he'd misled her before.

She cleared her throat. "Whatever, we've done a good job together."

"Right," he said.

They both went back to work. Paper rustled, computer keys clicked, but Ariel was constantly aware of Jeff only a few feet away—his movements, the occasional smile or chuckle as he read his mail, the scent of masculine shampoo and after-shave. She liked working in the same room with him. For a few moments, she let herself imagine doing this on a more permanent basis. Quiet weekends with working sessions interrupted by kisses, early-morning walks, heated discussions, heated love-making . . .

Suddenly she heard a choking sound. She looked up to see Jeff, an expression of horrified disbelief on his face, holding a pair of black briefs.

Ariel's mouth dropped open. She stood, took the briefs from him and held them up. "Hmm, interesting. See-through. I've never seen any quite like them before." She dropped them into his lap. "Can I read the letter?"

"What letter?"

"The one I smelled across the room."

He grabbed a sheet of hot-pink stationery that reeked of cologne and tore it to shreds. "Believe me, you don't want to know what it says." He tossed the paper in the trash. "That's enough."

"Jeff." Ariel tried to make her voice soothing. "Don't get so worked up over some silly letters. They're harmless."

"Harmless?" He shoved the box away. "You don't get it, do you?"

Puzzled, Ariel shook her head.

"Aren't you women always bitching about being viewed as sex objects? Don't you find it demeaning?"

"Yes, but—"

"What makes you think it's any different for a man?"

"I guess I've never thought of it," Ariel admitted.

"How do you think I feel," he continued, his voice thick with anger, "getting into an elevator and having a woman whisper, 'It's the hunk,' and start mentally undressing me? And another thing," he continued before she could reply, "all this half-baked hunk stuff is destroying my credibility at work."

Horrified, Ariel stared at him. "What do you mean?"

He gave his hair a frustrated swipe. "I'm a scientist. How can I maintain that image when my name keeps turning up in the papers as a sex symbol?"

"Jeff, I'm sorry. I didn't realize the repercussions for you."

"Keep them in mind from now on." She nodded, and he glanced at his watch. "I'd better go get ready." He left the room without saying goodbye.

THAT NIGHT, ARIEL dreamed about him. Her dreams were vivid—Jeff making wildly passionate love to her. And then doing it again. She woke, heated and trembling, the sheets twisted around her.

Her bedside clock read five-fifteen. Instead of trying to go back to sleep, Ariel got out of bed, repeated her affirmation for the day, then wandered outside and sat on the edge of her back deck, watching the night slip away. The sweet scent of dew-moistened grass wafted to her nostrils, the faintest whisper of a breeze touched her skin. Silence surrounded her. Here, with the colors of dawn brushing the sky and only a squirrel perched on the fence for company, she could cast aside her responsibilities and savor the peace and solitude. Rarely did she have time to stop and think about where she was heading; instead, she spent her days in a frantic race to get there.

She thought about Jeff and what he'd said yesterday and felt ashamed for not having given any thought to the effect on him of her casual suggestion that Heidi include him in her column. She'd been unfair, thinking only of herself and her need to win the contest.

She wanted Houston, she wanted success; but who would she share them with? She'd told Jeff she planned to have a family some day. Would she? Or would work consume her? Her brother Chad had fallen victim to the demands of his job. His marriage had ended because of it. Would she be any different? It seemed she was on an endless quest, moving from one station to the next, never staying anywhere long enough to settle in. For nearly a year now, she'd been concentrating on Houston—so much so that she'd barely made a home for herself in Corpus Christi. She didn't even have a deck chair. That made her feel lonely.

Her alarm buzzed from the bedroom behind her, and, with a sigh, she rose and went inside to get ready for the day.

Once she reached the office, her uncharacteristic pensive mood disappeared as she plunged into the frenetic activity of the station. At noon she attended a chamber-of-commerce luncheon where she was heartily congratulated for the hurricane series. She wished Jeff were there so he could share the compliments. Together, they were making a difference in the city.

She spent the afternoon conferring by telephone with a representative from the national chain with which the Foster stations were affiliated, drafting memos, answering letters. No, the station was not interested in a children's show featuring actors dressed like grasshoppers. No, they did not broadcast in Arabic. Yes, she'd be happy to cooperate with the police department on a Crime Stoppers feature.

She and Steve met in his office to determine which of the applicants for anchorwoman they'd invite for personal interviews. They settled on four, decided Steve would contact them and schedule the interviews for the following week. At six they decided to take a break. On the way to the soft-drink machine, they met Jeff and Kara coming into the building. Jeff lugged a sheet of plywood, Kara a box of tools.

Steve hurried to Kara. "Let me get that for you."

"Thanks. We've been shopping for Jeff's next show. He's talking about preparing houses before a storm blows in. Come on, I'll show you where this stuff goes."

Ariel ambled beside Jeff as he followed Steve and Kara. He'd been so angry yesterday, she wondered if he would have stopped in to talk to her if they hadn't bumped into each other.

"I wonder when Kara's going to wake up and notice he's crazy about her," Jeff said in a low voice.

Ariel stared at him. She didn't think he'd noticed Steve's severe case of unrequited love. "Some people are dense."

"They're so different from one another, but maybe we should give Kara a nudge," Jeff suggested. "Just a subtle one."

"*Some* people don't get subtlety. You have to beat them over the head." She stared pointedly at Jeff. He certainly fit in category number two. How could a man who looked like sex personified be so thickheaded? Didn't he realize how Ariel felt about him? No, she'd probably have to toss him to the ground and ravish him before he woke up to the fact that she was interested. And why was she, a woman who knew what she wanted and went after it, reluctant to make a move? Because, in this case, she *didn't* know what she wanted.

"If you're finished for the day, why don't we get a bite to eat?" he suggested, surprising her again.

"I'm finished," she said, mentally shoving her stack of still-unanswered mail out of sight. This was the first time Jeff had asked her out, and she intended to make the most of it.

THEY ATE AT LIN WAN, a cozy Cantonese restaurant near the station. Jeff's anger seemed to have abated, and Ariel wasn't about to bring up any dangerous topics. They laughed and chatted over spring rolls and almond chicken. When the fortune cookies arrived, Ariel broke hers open. "Have faith in yourself, and you can accomplish whatever you wish." She slipped it into her purse. Written in the first person, it would make a good affirmation for tomorrow. "What did yours say?"

"I didn't open it," Jeff answered. "I get enough fortune-telling at the office. My secretary's into astrology."

She'd noticed. "Come on, be a sport," Ariel urged. When he continued to refuse, she grabbed his cookie and opened it herself. "Laugh and the world laughs with you. Snore and you sleep alone," she read, giggling. "Do you snore?"

"No."

"Then I guess you don't have to—" The words stuck in her throat as his eyes darkened.

They stared at one another for a charged moment, then the waitress's voice broke the spell. "Y'all want your check?"

Jeff blinked. "Uh, yes."

After dinner Jeff drove along the beach. When they left the city behind them, he pulled over. "Let's take a walk."

Ariel slipped off her sandals, and they walked down to the cool sand. "The beach is different at night," she said, as she listened to the thunder of the waves and watched their ceaseless ebb and flow. Above them, away from the lights of the city, the sky seemed blacker. "It's more mysterious, more vast."

"And isolated."

"Doesn't that make you feel lonely?" she asked, remembering her early-morning mood.

He laughed and reached for her hand. "I can use a little loneliness. Since I've become a television personality, my life is like a three-ring circus." He gestured toward the water. "Here, I can get away from all the turmoil and be myself."

"Who are you, Jeff?" she asked softly.

He stopped and looked down at her. "Just a quiet guy."

He was that, she thought, but there was more. Layers and layers. He was as deep as the Gulf. "Is that what you want—quiet?"

"I'm not a hermit, Ariel, but I do like my privacy."

"Have you ever been married?"

"No. I was engaged once, but it didn't work out."

"Why?"

"Television came between us."

For a moment she thought he was joking, but then she looked into his eyes and saw that he was deadly serious. "I . . . I don't understand."

Jeff sighed and stared out to sea. "Several officers in the bank where my father was vice president were involved in a money-laundering scandal a few years ago. My dad wasn't one of them, but he was judged guilty by association. At least that's what the media thought. Wherever he went, wherever my mother went, there were microphones shoved in their faces, questions, innuendos. Elaine, my fiancée, wasn't happy." He laughed derisively. "You see, her father is a judge, and she had plans to run for Congress, so she didn't want to be associated with even the slightest taint of corruption. She broke our engagement."

Ariel felt her eyes well with tears at the emotion in his voice. She wanted to comfort him, to wipe the memories away. She put her free hand on his cheek. "That must have hurt."

He nodded. "As soon as the scandal broke, she began seeing someone else behind my back, a senator's son from Colorado. A more appropriate mate. Eventually, they married."

No wonder Jeff had such an aversion to television; no wonder he was so slow to trust. Ariel could think of nothing to say in the face of Elaine's betrayal, other than, "She was a fool."

Jeff gave a hollow laugh. "Some might say she was a politician." He bent, picked up a shell, and tossed it into the churning water. "I wouldn't have married Elaine no matter what, after I'd found out she'd been seeing someone else. How could I plan a lifetime with someone I couldn't trust?"

"I was engaged once, too," Ariel said after a while. "Just before I moved to Corpus."

He must have heard the tremor in her voice, for he tightened his hold on her hand. "What happened?"

As she spoke, she tried to sort it out for herself. In view of her mood this morning, the breakup of her engagement wasn't as clear-cut as it had always seemed. "I was living in Fort Worth and working as assistant manager of our station there. Keith and his brother owned a very successful chain of men's stores. He approached the station about doing some commercials, and I began working with him. We hit it off right away, and within six months we were engaged. Only he wanted me to quit working. He wanted someone who'd create a lovely home, give elegant parties, cultivate the right people."

"I can't imagine you staying home."

"You can't?"

He chuckled and squeezed her hand. "Hurricane Ariel? You'd drive the Junior League crazy."

"I said yes."

He stared at her. "I guess I misjudged you."

"No, *I* misjudged me. I wanted to make Keith happy. I was in love, or I thought so at the time."

"What changed your mind?"

"Circumstances. We hadn't told anyone about our plans yet, even our families. My dad called to tell me the manager of Channel 4 here had quit and the job was mine." She dropped Jeff's hand and turned away to stare at the pounding surf. Salt spray dampened her cheeks.

Standing behind her, he put his hands on her shoulders. "And?"

"And I realized I wanted the manager's job."

"More than you wanted to be a housewife."

"No," she said with a wry laugh. "I wanted both. I tried to convince Keith we could both have what we wanted. His company had opened stores in San Antonio and Austin. I suggested he open one in Corpus. Then he could manage the south Texas branch of the firm. I promised him I'd give him the home he wanted, the parties, the contacts, and still work." She sighed. "I knew it was a long shot, and I was right. No way would he leave Fort Worth. He wouldn't compromise, but then neither would I. I realized I wanted my career more than I wanted to be Keith's wife. But the breakup still hurt. If we'd told our folks earlier—"

"You'd have gotten married and lived unhappily ever after."

Warm fingers massaged her neck, easing the tension, erasing the memories. "You're probably right," she said.

They stood silently, each lost in thought. Then the roar of motorcycles roused them, and they turned to see a group of teenagers, laughing and talking, descending on the beach. "Hey, man. Here's a good spot."

"Let's party," someone shouted, and the sound of heavy metal burst from a boom box and shattered the stillness, drowning out the pounding of the waves and ending their quiet interlude.

They returned to the car and drove back to the station. Again Jeff walked her to her parking space. The lot was dark, almost deserted. When they reached her car, he put his hands on her shoulders. "I have to go to Florida for a couple of days to finalize a project. I'll see you Monday."

"Yes."

With gentle pressure, he pulled her closer. "We can get a bite after the newscast. Okay?"

"Okay."

He bent his head, pulling her closer still. Ariel's eyes fluttered closed.

Then his lips covered hers.

My God, she thought, as his mouth crushed hers and her legs went weak. This was no tender, tentative kiss. This was power and passion and wild, hot need. His lips seared hers, branded them. He kissed her until she forgot everything but the heat of his mouth, the strength of his arms. He could take her anywhere, any way, and she'd let him. No, she'd welcome him.

Ariel made herself focus on what had happened before, when he'd left her standing by her car—her confusion and hurt. And later, her anger.

This time, she was the one to walk away.

9

THE NEXT FEW DAYS Ariel and Steve met with candidates for the coanchor position. At the end of their fourth interview, Ariel glanced at her assistant, and Steve nodded. Wendy Norris was definitely the best of the applicants.

Wendy was tall and trim, with an air of confidence and the kind of face people wouldn't forget—wavy dark hair, large brown eyes, and a winning smile. She'd come across well on camera, and she and Hal would complement one another. "We're impressed, Wendy," Ariel said. "If you're interested, the job is yours."

"I'm interested."

Ariel named a starting salary.

"Definitely interested," Wendy said.

"We'd like you to begin as soon as possible. How about September first?" Wendy agreed, and Ariel smiled. "Wonderful. We'll have a contract drawn up right away. What do you say we celebrate over lunch? That'll give you a chance to meet Kara Taylor, the news-show producer, and Hal Monroe, our anchor."

Hal and Kara went in Hal's car, and Steve offered his. Ariel climbed into the back seat and watched Steve gallantly open the door for their guest. As they drove along the seawall, Wendy gazed past the palm trees to the sparkling water and the beachfront crowded with tanned sun-worshipers and less daring souls half-hidden beneath colorful umbrellas. She turned to Steve. "I can't wait to get down here and spend some time on the beach. Tell me, do you surf?"

"A little when conditions are right." Ariel was surprised. She'd had no idea Steve was a surfer. "Do you?" he asked.

"No chance for that in Abilene, but I'd love to learn. Or just come along and watch." She gave him a warm smile, and Steve basked in its glow. At the restaurant, he pulled out her chair and sat beside her. "What do you recommend?" she asked him.

"The pasta primavera." She ordered it.

Ariel ordered wine and proposed a toast. "To the newest member of the Channel 4 news team."

"To my coanchor," Hal added.

"To a long and productive association," Steve said, beaming at Wendy. Ariel blinked. Steve rarely made toasts.

During lunch Wendy said, "I'll have to look for a place to live. Any suggestions?"

Kara recommended a condo not far from the beach; Hal knew of a town house for sale in his neighborhood. Wendy turned to Steve. "Maybe you could help me look around."

He glanced at Kara, who was absorbed in her pasta. "Sure."

"I'll call you when I get in. We'll make plans."

A budding romance, Ariel thought. She wondered if anyone else noticed.

"DID YOU SEE HER?" Kara grumbled later in Ariel's office.

"Who?"

"Wendy Norris. Did you notice how she came on to Steve?"

Interesting, Ariel thought. She could have sworn Kara hadn't paid the slightest attention. "She seemed to like him."

"Like him? She was practically in his lap. 'What should I order, Steve? Maybe you could help me look around, Steve. We'll make plans.'" She huffed. "'Maybe I can move in with you, Steve.'"

"She didn't say that."

"But I bet she thought it."

Ariel suppressed a laugh. "Well, what's wrong with that? Steve's a big boy."

"And she's a barracuda."

"Come on, Kara." Ariel allowed herself a smile. "Steve can take care of himself."

Kara scowled and crossed her arms over her chest. "Can he? He's so sweet and gentle. He almost seems . . . innocent. She'll swallow him whole."

Ariel raised a brow. Oh, she was enjoying this. "Maybe he'd like being swallowed."

"Ha!"

"You know," Ariel said slyly, "lots of women find innocence in a man appealing."

"Do you?"

Thoughts of Jeff flashed into Ariel's mind. Innocent? Not the way he kissed.

"No, you like hunks, don't you?" Kara said with a knowing smile. "Tall, dark and brooding hunks."

Ariel blushed. "Anyway," she said, getting back to the subject at hand, "Steve isn't as sweet and innocent as he looks."

"He isn't?"

"Uh-uh."

Kara frowned. "How do you know?"

"I don't have firsthand knowledge," Ariel assured her hastily, "but I've heard women talk."

"Really?" Kara leaned forward, very interested now. "Who?"

"You know the newsperson's credo. I never reveal my sources." She watched the emotions flit across Kara's face—surprise, curiosity, even a flash of jealousy. Ariel leaned back in her chair. She'd given Kara that subtle nudge she and Jeff had discussed. Now it was up to the producer to follow through.

Kara wasn't one to procrastinate. She rose. "If we're finished, I need to run."

Following her out, Ariel watched as Kara strode purposefully toward Steve's office. She half opened the door and asked, "Can I talk to you for a minute?"

Ariel watched the door shut behind Kara and went back to her own office, chuckling to herself. Finally Kara's eyes had been opened. Sweet, gentle Steve was about to be pursued by a master of the chase. It would be interesting to see what happened next.

Meanwhile, Ariel went back to work. The phone rang. The governor would be in town tomorrow. Ariel called the news staff to be sure someone was available to follow the governor's itinerary.

Word of a five-car pileup on the freeway came in and a crew tore out of the building. Ariel could hear the sirens from her office. She went to the window and watched as the Channel 4 helicopter took off.

Perry Weston plodded in and informed her that thunderstorms were predicted over the weekend. "Is the hunk going to cover them?" he asked.

"*You're* going to cover them," she snapped. When Perry left, the phone rang. And rang again.

She continued working until nearly eleven. As late as it was when she arrived home, as sleepy as she was, she still couldn't help thinking about Jeff, wondering about his Florida trip. How had he spent his evening? Was there a woman in Florida? Or was he thinking of *her?* When she fell into bed at last, she shut her eyes and saw his face, relived their last kiss, and wondered what would happen the next time they were together.

AT SIX IN THE MORNING her alarm rang. Another whirlwind day began, and the pace never slackened. Mechanical problems with the helicopter, a cameraman injured covering the aftermath of a holdup, a news reporter down with a virus. Ariel could hardly find time to get a breath.

Even on the weekend, she had no time to relax. Saturday she addressed a meeting of the American Association of University Women, attended a dinner dance given by the Padre Island Tourist Association, and staggered home at two in the morning. The predicted thunderstorms finally arrived, and she stayed awake, huddling under the covers while thunder boomed and lightning flashed outside. By morning the thunder quieted, and she dragged herself out of bed.

Sunday was another busy day. She and Steve had their monthly breakfast meeting at The Coffee Shop, a café specializing in breakfasts and brunches. Today, Steve was preoccupied. "You're not paying attention," Ariel said crossly.

"My mind was on something else."

"What?" she asked, though she had a pretty good idea.

"Kara asked me out for tonight."

"Did she?" She scrutinized his face. "You don't look happy. Isn't this the answer to your prayers?"

He pushed the pancakes around on his plate. "Yeah, but now that she has, I can't figure out why. She said she wanted to talk about some ideas for the ten o'clock news, but I don't know. She's never asked me out to discuss business before. Maybe what she really wants is to talk to me about another guy—you know, that jock she's been seeing."

Ariel patted his hand. "Steve, my boy, *just maybe* she asked you over because she's interested in *you*."

He gave her a puzzled frown. "She never was before."

"But this is now. Trust me, Steve. She's probably realized you're a prize."

Now he looked hopeful. "Gosh, I wonder what I did to make her notice me."

You didn't do anything. You can thank Wendy Norris. Ariel merely shrugged and smiled at him. "Maybe you'll find out tonight."

After their meal, she went to the station for more work, which again lasted into the night. By Monday she felt like a sleepwalker, but she woke up enough to question Steve about his evening with Kara.

"It was nice," he said.

"Did she talk about the jock?"

"No. About work," he said. "But something was different. I don't know—the way she looked at me, like she'd never seen me before." A slow blush made its way from his cheeks to the roots of his red hair.

"Sounds promising," Ariel said, and resolved to get Kara's side of the story before the day was out.

She had an opportunity after lunch when the producer stopped by her office with some papers. "My sources tell me you spent the evening with Steve, discussing station business."

"Yeah. You know, I never realized how sexy Steve is . . . in a shy way."

"You have to watch out for those quiet ones," Ariel agreed, thinking of Jeff. "They're the sexiest of all."

After Kara left, Ariel attacked her mail. First, a letter from the network. A new show was premiering, a mystery with a healthy dose of sex. Spurred by declining ratings, they'd decided to move the debut up to August to test it out and to get a head start on the fall season. Great! Of course, Chad and Daniel would also benefit if the show turned out to be a hit, but *they* didn't have Jeff McBride, Ariel's ace in the hole.

She was pleased, but her energy was fading fast. She eyed the couch across the room. She wouldn't give it high marks for comfort, but it beat sitting at her desk. She clutched the pile of papers and carried them to the couch, kicked off her shoes and tucked her feet under her. Within minutes, the words before her blurred. She'd rest for a moment, she decided, dropping the papers to the floor.

"JEFF, GUESS WHAT!" Debra Tucker's eyes sparkled as she opened her door and gestured him inside. "Someone recognized me at the gas station last week."

Someone had recognized him, too—at the shoe-repair shop, at the drugstore, at the airport when he'd gotten off the plane from Tallahassee.

"Are you enjoying being a celebrity?" he asked.

"Aw, she's not *really* a celebrity," Travis said.

"Why, sure I am, honey."

"No way. You said a celebrity's like Madonna. People scream when they see her. Ain't nobody screamed at the gas station."

Debra frowned at *her* son. "Don't say 'ain't.'"

"*Didn't* nobody scream at the gas station."

Debra rolled her eyes.

"But they did know who she was," Jeff argued. "How'd you feel, Debra?"

"It was a kick! And don't let Travis kid you? He liked it, too. He strutted around over his famous mom."

Jeff couldn't say *he* liked being famous. He'd begun wearing sunglasses, but that hadn't prevented a couple of young women from spotting him the other day and practically swooning at his feet. "Listen, Travis. By the end of the day, you'll be a celebrity, too. The new Macaulay Culkin."

The boy's eyes widened. "No shi—"

"Travis!" Debra gave him a shocked look. "Say 'Excuse me.'" She grimaced. "I don't know where he picks up that language."

"Excuse me," Travis said. "No kidding?"

"Would I kid you? Today your mother and I are going to talk about how to tell children about hurricanes."

"Don't you just say, 'A storm's comin' and you better hide. It might blow down the house'?"

"Like the Big Bad Wolf?" four-year-old Tammy asked. "It'll huff and puff and blow your house down." She giggled with delight and demonstrated huffing and puffing.

"That's not quite how we're going to handle it," Jeff said.

"Yeah. Some kids don't know as much about hurricanes as y'all do," Debra said. "Some kids might be scared."

"They're 'fraidy cats," Mark scoffed.

"Today we're going to teach them about storms so they won't be 'fraidy cats," Jeff said, and when the camera rolled, he began. "The idea that a violent storm may hit your home can be terrifying. Children can be doubly frightened. Psychologist Dr. Don Carroll says you should talk to your kids if a storm is imminent. Today Debra Tucker and her family will show us how."

JEFF REACHED THE TV station barely in time for his makeup session. He hoped Ariel would drop by and was disappointed when she didn't. She wasn't in the control booth during his live segment, either. As soon as he was done, he went in search of her.

He'd thought about her too much since he'd left. And at the most inappropriate times. During lunch with the crotchety department head at Florida State, someone at the table behind them had laughed and he'd thought of Ariel—her eyes bright with mischief. In the midst of a meeting, the secretary had come in with a computer printout and he'd caught a whiff of her perfume, which reminded him of the exotic, musky fragrance Ariel wore. He'd shifted uncomfortably, afraid his body was advertising the direction his mind had taken. And at night, alone in his hotel room, he had pictured making love with Ariel all night long.

Now he strode down the hall toward her office. Her secretary smiled nervously, doubtless remembering his assault on the office several weeks ago. "She's in."

"Thanks." He opened the door and went inside. At first he assumed the room was empty. Then he saw her on the couch.

She slept deeply, curled up like a child, her head pillowed on her hand. Her golden hair fell in a soft curtain over her cheek. He longed to smooth her hair away, kiss her cheek, trace the fine blue veins in her hand.

Instead, he watched her, enthralled. He'd never seen her still before. Always she'd been a whirlwind of activity. Now the gentle rise and fall of her breathing was her only movement.

He stepped closer, his eyes following the curves of her breasts, her hips, down her slim legs to small feet with pink-painted toenails peeking through sheer stockings. He longed to sweep her into his arms, carry her away, and ignite her passion . . . and his.

She sighed in her sleep and curled her arms around herself as if she might be cold. Jeff noticed her jacket draped over the back of her desk chair and went to get it. He held the jacket to his face and took a breath. It carried her scent. He went to the couch and knelt beside her. He tucked the jacket around her shoulders, and she stirred.

Sleepy eyes opened and stared, startled, into his. Sleeping Beauty, and he'd awakened her with a touch. "Jeff," she whispered, and lifted her hand to his cheek. "I was dreaming about you."

"Were you?" He wondered if her dreams were as erotic as his.

"When did you get here?" she asked.

"While ago," he murmured, caught in the sea blue depths of her eyes. "I wanted to see you." But seeing wasn't enough. He leaned closer and kissed her. With his tongue he traced the outline of her lips, then dipped between them into the warm recesses of her mouth.

He pushed aside the jacket that covered her. His hand trailed across her throat, then downward to her breast. He stroked its softness, felt the nipple stiffen, and bent his head to kiss it through the silky material of her blouse.

He'd only meant to kiss her, only meant to touch her, but she moaned, and the sound shattered his control. He tossed her jacket to the floor, and leaned over her. His hands worked rapidly at the buttons of her blouse, slid the camisole down and freed her breasts. His tongue caressed her dusky nipples and his desire grew fierce as she moaned his name again and again in a litany of desire. He wanted her now, here on the cramped couch, with her computer blinking in the background and God-knew-who a yard away in the next office.

"I want you," he groaned, his hand splaying over her hip. "God, I want you." He tugged at the zipper on her skirt—and heard the sound of laughter from the other side of the door.

No, not here. This was a spot for quickie sex, not for making love. Clenching his teeth with the effort to hold back, he raised his head. He took a breath, brushed a strand of golden hair from Ariel's cheek. "Come home with me," he whispered hoarsely.

"Yes," she answered and gave him her hand.

He pulled her to her feet and back into his arms. He pressed her against him, feeling her softness. He wondered how he'd waited so long. He wondered how he could wait any longer.

What had just happened—what would happen later— was inevitable. Like a slowly building storm, desire that had been spawned at their first meeting had escalated, and now raged beyond their control. Tonight he would take Ariel to his bed. He could already hear the thunder.

10

ARIEL TURNED TO GAZE at Jeff as they walked, arms
around each other, through the lobby of his high-rise
building. In the elevator, he backed her into the corner
and kissed her hard. She clutched his shoulders, breathless, half dizzy with delight and desire, wondering if this
wasn't a fantasy of her imagination.

Then, suddenly, he tore his lips away. "I think we've
stopped." Had they? She hadn't noticed.

Seconds later, he unlocked the door of his apartment
and flicked on the light. "Would you, um, like to have a
drink?"

Had the man who'd kissed her so passionately in the
elevator turned shy? No, she decided, glancing at him.
He was trying to put *her* at ease. "Uh-uh," she said,
laughing softly. "I'd rather have you."

"Thank God. One minute longer and I'd..." He
opened his arms and she stepped into them, feeling as if
she'd come home. He kissed her for a long moment,
swept her up in his arms, and carried her into his bedroom. He laid her on the bed, then stretched out beside
her. He kissed her forehead, her eyelids. His tongue circled her ear.

While his lips roamed her face, he unfastened her
clothing, his hands as sure as if he knew every button.
Within minutes, she lay naked, exposed to his burning
gaze. No man had ever looked at her with such fierce
hunger.

She wanted to see him, too. All of him. She rose to her knees and faced him, pulled his shirt free and worked at the buttons, her fingers faltering as Jeff diverted her with warm, wet kisses along her shoulders, between her breasts. "You're distracting me."

"Mmm." He took her nipple into his mouth, suckling deeply.

She gasped and clutched his shoulders. When he pulled her against him, she sighed at the warmth of his chest. His hands moved slowly down from her shoulders, along the column of her spine, then cupped her bottom and drew her even closer.

"I've been dreaming of this since I first saw you, when you stormed into my office," he whispered between kisses. "I thought you were beautiful."

Ariel nibbled at his jaw. "I thought you were a jerk."

Jeff stopped mid-kiss. *"What?"*

She rained kisses over his chest. "A gorgeous, sexy jerk." Half laughing, he started to pull back, but she held him fast. She unzipped his trousers and tugged them down, then trained her gaze on the arousal straining against his briefs. "Mmm, I was right. You are definitely sexy."

He laughed hoarsely. "You don't give a man much choice." Then he caught her hands and held them. "And am I a jerk, too?"

"Nope, for a change I was wrong." She cupped her hands around him and stroked him through his briefs. He caught his breath.

A moment later, when her lips followed her hands, he groaned and pulled her away. "We have to…slow down. I can't…wait."

"Then don't." She slid her hands beneath the waistband of his briefs and dragged them down.

He kicked them off, and there were no more teasing words. Only gasps from both of them as he plunged inside her. Only sighs, moans, and ragged breaths. They moved together, faster, racing madly toward the end.

Wild with pleasure, delirious with love, Ariel wanted to experience everything—the taste of his mouth, the texture of his skin, the faint scent of the makeup he'd worn earlier, the ripple of his muscles as he moved against her—but she couldn't sort them out. Emotions and sensations merged, swelled; and she was swept into a realm she'd never experienced before. Nothing in her dreams or her imagination had prepared her for this. The pleasure too much to bear, she reached a shattering climax, and, with a hoarse cry, Jeff followed her.

Slowly, gradually, they settled—breathing calmed, heartbeats slowed. Ariel opened her eyes. "Are we back on Earth?"

"I think so."

"Wherever we were, I've never been there before."

"It was like flying into a hurricane." He kissed her softly, touched her tongue with his. "Hurricane Ariel."

They lay quietly for a while. With a finger, Jeff traced the line of her brow, the curve of her lips. "Why did you think I was a jerk?"

"Oh, dear. Are you still worried about that?"

"Just curious."

She rose up on an elbow. "I had such a good idea, and you didn't want to listen."

"Is everyone who ignores your ideas a jerk?" he teased.

She bent to kiss his nose. "Of course not, but I was frustrated. I wanted you for the show, but I think I was attracted to you, too, and you were making it hard for me."

He laughed. "And now you've returned the favor." He took her hand and placed it on himself. She felt his hard, pulsing arousal.

"So soon?"

"Like a hurricane," he said, lifting her so that she lay above him. "First there's the storm." Lazily, he began tracing circles on her back with a fingertip. "Next you have the eye, when everything's quiet, then the storm again."

"I see." Ariel smiled. "What's the forecast?"

"We'd better brace ourselves," Jeff said. "The second half's about to start." He slipped inside her, and they flew again.

Later, as Ariel lay locked in Jeff's arms, listening to the even sounds of his breathing, she knew she'd never be the same. *They'd* never be the same. What had happened tonight in this bed had been more than physical.

ARIEL WOKE BY DEGREES. With eyes still closed, she felt the sunlight streaming through the window, the warmth of Jeff's body beside her. Then she heard a whirring sound at her ear, as if someone had turned on a miniature motor. Surely that tiny sound wasn't Jeff's alarm clock.

She opened her eyes and stared into a pair of glittering green ones. The sound she heard came from the throat of a large white cat stretched out by her shoulder. "Hello, kitty," she said.

On the other side of her, Jeff stretched. "Blizzard?"

With a noisy meow, the cat stepped gracefully over Ariel, parked itself on Jeff's chest, and resumed purring.

"Your roommate?" Ariel asked, reaching over to stroke the animal's silky white fur.

"Yeah. I guess he decided to give us some privacy last night." Jeff rubbed the cat's head, and the purrs increased in volume. Ariel understood how Blizzard felt. His owner was a master at pleasure giving.

Jeff turned to nuzzle Ariel's ear. "Want some breakfast?"

"Mmm-hmm." She sat up. "Do you have orange juice?"

"Grapefruit."

She frowned and leaned over to plant a smacking kiss on his cheek. "Orange has more vitamin C."

"I'll put it on my shopping list. Meanwhile, I'll see if I can scrounge up something healthy." He removed the cat from his chest and sat up.

Ariel peered at the dress Jeff had helped her discard last night. It lay on the floor in a wrinkled heap. "Do you have a robe I can borrow?" she asked.

Jeff's gaze raked over her. "How about breakfast in the nude?"

"That sounds like one of Candy's ideas."

"Whose?"

"You remember. Thirty-six twenty-four thirty-eight. She wrote you a fan letter. Did you two get together?"

With a mock growl, Jeff grabbed her and pinned her beneath him. "You know better," he said, covering her face with kisses. The cat gave a disgusted meow, jumped off the bed, and stalked to the door. "Let's skip breakfast," Jeff suggested, trailing his lips along Ariel's shoulder.

"Never skip meals, McBride. That's one of my rules. Now be a good boy and get me something to wear."

"You're a tough lady, Foster." Sighing, he got up. He pulled on a pair of jeans, then went to his dresser and returned carrying a gray T-shirt with Carpe Diem emblazoned across the chest in red.

"'Seize the day,'" Ariel translated. "I approve." She slipped the shirt over her head and stood. "A bit long." The shirt reached her knees.

"But, God, you look sexy." His eyes darkened. "Sure you don't want to skip breakfast just this once?" He stepped closer.

"Don't tempt me."

"What about the exception that proves the rule?"

Ariel laughed. "My words are coming back to haunt me. Seriously, I have to get in early. Another time, maybe..."

He caught her arm and pulled her close. "No maybes."

She stood on tiptoe and kissed his cheek. "Definitely." Then she slipped away from him and went into the bathroom. She stared at her face in the mirror. Her eyes glowed. The faint trace of a love bite showed on her neck. She looked like a woman who had been thoroughly and expertly loved. She sighed. How had she ever convinced herself that Jeff was no more than a way out of Corpus, nothing but a friend?

She was in love with him. He hadn't said anything about his feelings, but actions spoke louder than words—didn't they? His actions last night had been those of a man besotted. *Don't think about the future,* she warned herself. *Enjoy what you have, and maybe tomorrow will take care of itself.*

When she finished in the bathroom, she headed for the kitchen and the aroma of breakfast. But in the living room, she caught sight of the view from the plate-glass window and stopped. "I didn't notice this last night. How lovely."

The room overlooked the blue-gray expanse of the Gulf where early-morning sunlight shimmered across the water, streaking it with gold. Gulls wheeled above the shore, white against the cloudless sky. A boat skimmed over the waves, its sails a palette of dawn colors.

Ariel opened the sliding door and stepped onto the balcony, drawing in a deep breath of salty air. "You're lucky to live up here," she called over her shoulder. "It must be like seeing a painting every morning. So beautiful."

He stepped out behind her and pulled her back against his chest. "Even more beautiful with you here." He bent his head to brush a kiss over her temple. "Will you come back tonight?"

"Yes— Oh, heck. It's the news team's monthly bowling night. Want to come with us, and then we'll . . . ?"

"Make love. Yes."

They shared a breakfast of scrambled eggs and toast, then Ariel drove home to change clothes. On the way, she made a mental note to bring some granola with her for tomorrow—enough for both of them. She'd have to persuade Jeff to watch his cholesterol intake.

At home, she glanced at her bike, then decided to skip her morning exercise routine. Jeff had given her more than enough exercise last night. If things continued as she hoped, she might get rid of the bike entirely.

LATE THAT EVENING Jeff pulled up at the bowling alley. Although bowling was far from his favorite sport, he'd looked forward to this all day. He hurried inside the building.

It was crowded and noisy. The sound of rolling balls and crashing pins echoed around him. Cigarette smoke hung in the air. Bowlers in gaudy shirts with team names such as Lucky Strikes and Alley Cats occupied the lanes. He made his way through the raucous crowd until he saw the Channel 4 group at two of the lanes.

Ariel spotted him and waved, and he hurried toward her. With her hair tied back in a ponytail, she looked like a teenager. She wore jeans and a yellow, green and orange shirt that sported the Channel 4 logo and the name StriKCORps, which he deciphered to mean "Strike Corps."

"Jeff," Hal Monroe said, holding out a hand. "Glad you're here. We need a sub. Are you a bowler?"

"Sure." He could use the activity to keep his mind off…other things. He'd looked at Ariel for no more than a moment, but her slow, secret smile had gone straight to his loins. He hoped this bowling business didn't last too long. He wanted her alone, naked in his arms, her hands on his—

"Balls," Hal said.

"Huh?"

"I said, you'll find the bowling balls right over there," the anchor replied.

"Oh, right. I'll need shoes, too," Jeff mumbled and went to get outfitted.

When he returned, Hal introduced his wife Janelle, a small, dark-eyed woman, who was also substituting tonight. The two of them, Jeff and Ariel made up one team. Kara, Steve and two news reporters were on the other team. Jeff was surprised to see that Kara was seated beside Steve and was quite obviously making a play for him. Jeff nudged Ariel and gestured toward the two, who were so absorbed in each other, they couldn't have noticed. "What happened?" he whispered.

"Jealousy. Powerful stuff."

Jeff nodded. Whoever had made Kara jealous, she hadn't wasted any time staking a claim. Judging from the look on Steve's face, she had him totally under her spell.

"You're up first, Ariel," Hal informed her.

She picked up her ball, tested its weight, then narrowed her eyes, and nailed a strike. "Yes!" Fist in the air, she swung around in triumph, then swaggered back to the bench.

For the rest of the evening, Jeff watched her in fascination. As she had done during the volleyball game on the Fourth of July, she put everything into this competition. After the match was over, as he and Ariel walked to their cars, he said, "You sure play hard. You'd think this was a national tournament, not a friendly match between co-workers.

"Competing's in my blood," Ariel told him. "Dad was a star running back for the Texas Longhorns, and he inspired that same kind of drive in us kids. He was always giving us pep talks—you know, 'Be the best you can be.' We competed for everything from grades to athletic trophies."

"Didn't that create conflict between you and your brothers?"

"No. Dad also taught us to be good losers. Sportsmanship was important."

"How'd you come out in the contests? Aren't you the youngest?"

"Yeah, and a girl, and the smallest. But you'd be surprised. I had my share of wins." She grinned. "I could swim more laps than anyone, jump a horse better, and I had the best grades in English. Chad couldn't write worth a darn, and Daniel was more interested in science." They reached Ariel's car, and she got in. "See you in ten minutes."

As he drove, Jeff thought about what Ariel had said. Creating rivalry between your children seemed odd to him; but, being an only child, maybe he didn't understand. Still, he couldn't picture his own father doing that, even if he'd had a dozen kids. He could see how competition had made Ariel the woman she was today, but the idea made him uncomfortable. Ariel's competitiveness and ambition bothered him. He pondered why as he drove. Was it because he saw these traits as emblematic of the media machine, especially television? Or was the blind single-mindedness of competition what disturbed him? A single-mindedness he had come face-to-face with in Ariel—more often than he liked.

But when he pulled into his garage, with Ariel right behind him, he pushed that thought aside and concentrated on the night to come. Ariel parked in a visitor's spot and, by the time he reached her, was lifting a large brown paper sack from the trunk.

"Let me get that," Jeff said. "Good Lord, what do you have in here, leftover bowling balls?"

"Nope. You'll find out in a minute." She grabbed an overnight bag and slung the strap over her shoulder.

Upstairs, Jeff put the paper bag on the kitchen counter. Blizzard jumped up and eyed the sack expectantly. Jeff shooed him back and reached in. "Granola."

"For breakfast."

Fresh-squeezed orange juice, a cantaloupe, and a jar of wheat germ came out, then a box of kitty snacks.

"Cat treats," Jeff said.

"And there are other treats to come." Her smile was sly.

"What kind of treats?"

"You'll see." She waved the package in Blizzard's direction.

"Meow." The cat rubbed against her legs.

"The way to a man's heart is through his cat," Ariel declared. "May I?" When Jeff nodded, she fed several goodies to Blizzard.

Jeff continued emptying the bag. Herbal tea, a lemon— "Holy cow!" He pulled out a wisp of nylon and lace. "What's this?"

"I told you there were more treats."

"If this is for breakfast, let's have it now."

She grabbed the nightie from him. "*This* is for tonight. Why don't we get you comfortable first?"

"Comfortable?" he echoed thickly. No way could he be comfortable thinking about that scrap of material and what it did—or didn't—cover.

She laughed throatily, took his hand and led him into the bedroom. "Soft music," she murmured and turned on his bedside radio. "Here we are. KCOR Radio—Easy Listening." The sounds of Whitney Houston filled the room.

"Now the bed," she said. Jeff helped her remove the spread, then she glided toward him seductively. "And now you." She undid his tie, tossed it aside, and slowly unbuttoned his shirt. Already aroused and impatient, he tried to push her hands away, but she shook her head. "I want to undress you. I want to get you ready."

He laughed hoarsely. "If I get any readier, I'll explode."

"No, you won't." She slipped the shirt from his shoulders and let it fall to the floor, then urged him down on the bed. "Just relax," she said, her voice a lazy purr. "Let me have my way with you."

He'd let her do anything...*anything*. He lay back and luxuriated in the pleasure she gave him. She continued to seduce him, tantalizing him with butterfly-soft kisses, fingertip-light caresses. Pulling his trousers down, inch by inch. Pausing to nip at his skin or lave it with her tongue. Retreating, lingering to look at him, her gaze hot as noon, her eyes dark as night. "I'm treating you like a sex object," she whispered. "Do you mind?"

Mind? He was half crazy with delight. This was a sexual fantasy come to life, and he was entranced. "I can take it," he panted.

No woman had made him ache this way; but no woman was Ariel. Dizzy with need, he sat up and reached for her, but she backed away. "Wait," she whispered, then bent to pick up the gown and, letting it trail behind her, glided away.

In a moment, he heard the shower go on in the bathroom. He was tempted to join her, but he couldn't make himself move. Besides, this was her show. He lay on the bed, waiting, wanting, while Ariel took her time.

When she finally opened the door, Jeff lost his breath. She was every man's fantasy in a gown designed to drive any man out of his mind. Black like midnight, like magic, it clung to her like a soft shadow. Two thin straps drew his eyes from the smooth ivory of her shoulders to her small, high breasts, their rosy tips peeking through a layer of lace, beckoning him to taste and touch. Filmy nylon skimmed her thighs and left her legs bare. She'd brushed out her hair so that it framed her face like a golden halo.

He rose and went to her, took her in his arms. The gown left her back bare to the waist. Her skin felt like satin, and she smelled like sin. He wanted her with a need that was almost painful, but he resolved to take his time, to give her the same agonizing pleasure she'd brought him. He carried her to the bed and cradled her in his arms, kissing her through the lace. Even the flimsy barrier between them was too much. He drew the straps down and freed her breasts, laving, then sucking each nipple in turn. Then he slipped the gown down over her hips, his hands tracing her hipbones, her thighs.

She murmured and moaned, then cried out when he found her hot, moist core. Loving the way she fit in his arms, loving the soft cries she made, he lingered there, arousing her with his fingers, until she tightened around his hand, then shattered with a cry. He held her until the spasms died away and she relaxed in his arms.

"Jeff, you didn't—"

"I will now." He turned her to face him, her legs straddling him, and he drove into her. He couldn't hold back. One fierce thrust, then another, and he exploded inside her.

Afterward, they tumbled to the bed, sated, too exhausted to talk, to move. But soon they recovered and repeated the experience. Several times.

FROM THEN ON, THEY spent every night together.

After his broadcast the next week Jeff was in Ariel's office, waiting for her to finish for the day when Hal Monroe stuck his head in. "Big news," he said.

Ariel beckoned him in, but the anchor looked pointedly at Jeff. "It's okay," she said. "Go ahead."

"There's more to the dirty work at St. Elizabeth's Hospital than we thought," he announced.

At the newsman's words, Jeff felt a flutter in his stomach. "Dirty work" of what kind? From whose point of view? That same term had been used in connection with his father's bank.

"Tell me," Ariel urged, her eyes glowing with excitement.

"More than one trustee is involved," Hal answered. "Three members of the board have an interest in the corporation that owned the land where the children's wing is going up."

"You have hard evidence?"

"Yep, enough to blow this thing sky-high. Three sources confirmed what I just told you. And that's not all the story. These guys are funneling lucrative construction contracts to firms that happen to be owned by relatives. Haven't bothered with bids or anything, just kept those multimillion-dollar deals in the family. And, yes, I can back that up, too."

The flutter in Jeff's stomach became a searing pain. He wished he hadn't stayed to hear this conversation. He watched Ariel's reaction.

"Let's get it on the air." Gone was the soft, throaty voice of his lover. In its place was the hard-edged excitement of a journalist in hot pursuit of a sensationalistic exposé.

Anger surged through Jeff as he noted her smile of satisfaction. Anger at Ariel, disgust with himself. He'd done what he'd promised himself he never would: gotten involved with this woman, who represented everything he despised. It was time for him to put an end to this affair; time to call it quits.

11

BEFORE HE LEFT, he'd tell Ariel what he thought. As soon as Hal shut the door, Jeff said, "So you have your scandal to liven up the summer."

"Looks like it." His sarcasm was apparently lost on her.

"And how many innocent people will be hurt because of it?"

Ariel frowned. "None. You heard Hal. He's not basing this story on conjecture. He has it on good authority—three sources."

"Your sources are only as good as their own principles. How do you know what their motives are?"

"That's why we don't rely on only one source." Ariel's tone was patient. "That's why we get confirmation."

Jeff swore and got out of his chair to pace the room. "You media people are all alike. You trust your sources because you want to, because there's something in it for you. Your news team will be after those trustees and their families like a pack of jackals. You don't give a damn how many people are hurt as long as you get your sound bites."

"This isn't about St. Elizabeth's Hospital, is it?" Ariel said quietly. "It's about your father."

"Damn right," he retorted. "There were sources in Tulsa, too, sources who wanted to shift the blame to an innocent man. He left the bank; he couldn't continue associating with people who'd almost framed him. But no other bank would hire him. Even though he wasn't indicted, he'd been tried and convicted on prime-time news. Two years went by before he was hired by a small suburban bank. The scandal that was such a coup for the television stations nearly ruined my father's life."

"I'm sorry, Jeff. Maybe the newspeople in Tulsa were careless. Hal is not, or he wouldn't be working for KCOR. The Foster stations don't go in for tabloid journalism. We're very, very cautious in what we say."

He leaned against the wall and glared at her. "Maybe you *think* you are."

"I *know* we are. Trust me, Jeff."

"I can't." The words hurt him as much as he could see they hurt Ariel. He turned away.

"So you're going to damn me and my whole profession because of one lousy TV station? People still listen to meteorologists, even though sometimes their predictions are wrong." Her voice came from directly behind him.

He swung around to face her. "It's not the same thing."

"It's close enough. Look, my folks are coming in next week before they go on vacation. I want you to meet them and see what kind of people they are, what kind of man my father is. I want you to hear how he runs his stations. All right?"

"I doubt he could convince me." He headed for the door.

She grabbed his arm. "Don't go." He turned back to look at her. Her mouth was set in a grim line. "I'm not going to beg you, but I think you owe me a chance to prove my integrity."

Her plea pierced the armor he'd drawn around him, but he didn't answer.

She drew a ragged breath. "Jeff, don't let this situation with the hospital spoil what's between us."

He stared at her silently, while her hand gripped his arm as if she'd never let go, while bitter memories warred with newfound passions. With a painful effort, he seized the hand that clasped him.

He meant to push her away, he *wanted* to push her away. But somehow he found himself pulling her closer, into his arms. She clung to him and he held her and kissed her. How could he give her up because of the work she did? He pressed her closer, buried his face in the golden silk of her hair, drank in her scent. No, he couldn't give her up—not now, not yet. He lifted her into his arms and carried her to the couch. This time he couldn't wait, *she* couldn't wait. They needed each other *now*.

THE STORY ON St. Elizabeth's broke the following evening. Hal Monroe handled it in low-key fashion. The trustees who were involved were given an opportunity to comment. Of course, none did. Jeff watched the story develop. If anyone was hounding the trustees and their families, it wasn't Channel 4. In fact, he admitted to Ariel, Hal's coverage had been fair and unbiased.

"You'll feel even better after you've met Dad," Ariel assured him the day her parents were to arrive.

Jeff's first impression of Ariel's father was of size. A broad, muscular man with silver-gray hair, Martin Foster could have been a football coach or a truck driver. "Glad you could join us," he said, extending a large hand, his shrewd eyes sizing Jeff up.

"And this is my mother, Virginia."

This was how Ariel would look in later years—the blond hair highlighted with silver, the soft skin, the waist only slightly thicker. Virginia was still attractive enough to draw a man's eyes. "It's a pleasure to meet you, Jeff," she said in a throaty voice like her daughter's.

They went to the Alhambra Room, which featured dining and dancing. "So, Jeff, how are you enjoying television?" Martin Foster asked as the waiter served their shrimp cocktails.

Jeff exchanged glances with Ariel. "It's been . . . an experience."

"Jeff's been watching the hospital scandal," Ariel remarked.

"Ah, yes. What do you think?"

He wasn't about to tell Martin Foster what he thought. Jeff was much more interested in learning how Foster felt. "It's an unfortunate situation if the rumor is true," he said.

Foster nodded. "Trustees playing fast and loose with hospital funds is a damned rotten shame. I'm proud of your news team, Ariel, for alerting the public. Even prouder of the way you're handling the story."

"Thanks, Dad. Jeff is interested in how we handle our coverage of something this inflammatory," Ariel said.

"Fair coverage," Martin answered. "That's our policy. Report the news, don't influence it."

Jeff nodded. He'd learned that Ariel's news team was nothing like the Tulsa reporters who'd been at his father like animals circling their prey.

Martin reached for his drink, took a sip, and gave Jeff a level look. "Ariel tells me you had some unpleasant experiences with the media in the past. I'm sorry to hear it. The TV stations in your hometown have the reputation of being scandalmongers. We're not like that. If one of my news reporters tried that, he'd be out on his ass."

"I'm glad to hear that," Jeff said, but he wondered if Martin was mouthing platitudes to impress him. Clearly,

Ariel had told him how Jeff felt about TV; saying the right thing would be easy. But in view of the way Channel 4 had been handling the hospital situation, he was at least willing to give Foster the benefit of the doubt.

"Tell me about the hurricane series," Martin said.

"Jeff's gotten a warm reception from viewers," Ariel interjected.

"Ah, yes," Martin said, "the hu—"

Ariel coughed.

"The, uh, hurricane expert. Think we'll have a big one this summer?"

"Good chance," Jeff replied.

"Jeff's talked to KCOR Radio," Ariel said, "and made plans to broadcast cooperatively if a storm hits. He's been meeting with the Emergency Planning Commission, too. He's given them some good ideas." She beamed at Jeff.

She was showing him off to her father, Jeff thought, feeling uncomfortable. Did she think of him as a new pet? *See what neat tricks he can do.*

To his relief, she changed the subject. "Oh, I forgot to tell you. The San Antonio chapter of Women in Communications has invited me to be the keynote speaker at their annual conference in September. I'll be speaking at the breakfast meeting."

They all congratulated her. While they'd been talking, the combo had begun to play. "Ginny," Martin said to his wife, "I think this is our dance."

Jeff and Ariel followed them to the tiny dance floor. "What was your father about to say when you interrupted him?" Jeff asked.

"Who knows?"

Jeff leaned back and peered into her innocent-looking blue eyes. "You know."

Ariel took a breath. "He was about to call you a hunk."

Jeff burst out laughing.

"You're not mad?"

"No," he said, still chuckling. "I'm getting used to crazy things."

"What did you think of Dad's philosophy of news coverage?"

"It sounds fine—in theory," he said.

"I'm going to prove to you that it works in fact."

"I hope you do," he said. He'd like nothing better than to trust Ariel implicitly, get off this roller coaster he was on—of not quite trusting her but needing her, wanting her, all the same. He sighed and pulled her closer.

When the music stopped, Martin extended a hand to his daughter. "Come show off with your old man."

Ariel winked at Jeff. "Dad always treats his station managers to dinner and dancing."

"I only dance with the pretty ones," Martin said.

"Mrs. Foster?" Jeff invited.

"I'd love to." When the music started again, they chatted amiably, then Virginia said, "I'm glad to see that Ariel's found a . . . friend."

Jeff's eyes wandered to Ariel, in conversation with her father. "She's a special person."

"It does a mother's heart good to hear that." Virginia sighed and looked at him closely. "But you know, I worry about her sometimes. She always seems on top of the world, but she has a lonely side to her, too."

"I've noticed." He'd seen glimpses of that loneliness when they'd talked on the beach, even at the Fourth of July picnic. He wondered why someone as outgoing as Ariel should be lonely.

The dance number ended, and the combo swung into something fast. Jeff and Virginia started back to their ta-

ble, then stopped when they saw Ariel and Martin still
on the floor.

Jeff was captivated by the way Ariel moved—picking
up the rock-tune rhythm, swaying, twisting, she seemed
a part of the music. "She could have been a dancer," Jeff
murmured.

"She had years of ballet and tap," Virginia said, smiling fondly. "Her father's no slouch on the dance floor,
either."

Jeff agreed. For a big man, Martin was surprisingly
agile. He and Ariel were now the center of attention.
Most of the other couples stopped to watch and clap
along to the rock beat. When the song ended, Ariel and
her father got a round of applause.

Both grinning, they returned to the table. Ariel might
look like her mother, Jeff decided, but she had her father's smile.

"This one wins the dance contest," Martin said, giving Ariel a pat.

"Contest with whom?" she asked. "The other station
managers?"

"My other children."

"Oh, pooh. You've never danced with Chad or Daniel. How would you know?" But she basked in her father's praise.

During the meal Ariel asked, "Mom, why did you two
decide to go to the beach in Mexico instead of Galveston?"

"For a change," Virginia said. To Jeff, she explained,
"We have a beach house in Galveston, but we don't use
it as much as we did when the children were home."

"It's a wonderful house," Ariel said. "A big blue three-
story right on Pirate's Beach, with white wicker furniture and decks all around. Chad and Daniel used to climb

down from the third-floor deck when they were in high
school and sneak out to some of the clubs along the
beach."

"Really?" Martin Foster questioned. When Ariel nodded, he said, "They were damn lucky I didn't catch them
then, or they'd have gotten their backsides paddled, big
as they were."

"I miss the days when you were all at home," Virginia
said. "We used to ride the ferry to Bolivar Island, go sailing...."

"I hated sailing," Ariel remarked. "It made me
queasy." Both parents looked astonished. Jeff was surprised, too. Ariel had joined him on the Gormans' boat
one weekend and had seemed enthusiastic during the
outing.

"But you were such a good sailor," Virginia protested.

"I had to force myself." Ariel looked at her father.
"Sailing was important to everyone else."

The conversation ended, but it stayed in Jeff's mind.
He'd thought Ariel's competitiveness and drive were in-
grained; now he wondered if they were born of an intense need to please her father. Martin Foster was a
formidable man. Jeff suspected the ex-jock wouldn't have
been pleased when his daughter became seasick, so she'd
conquered it. And he could easily picture Martin Foster
setting up competitions among his kids.

Later that night, while he and Ariel lay in his bed,
cuddled close, he asked, "Why did you learn to sail?"

"I told you," she said sleepily, "everyone else did."

"Why didn't you stay home?"

"I'd have disappointed everyone."

"Everyone? Or your father?"

"The whole family," she insisted. "What difference
does it make?"

"Why didn't you satisfy yourself rather than worry about pleasing your father?"

Ariel stiffened and sat up. "Don't be ridiculous," she said, keeping her back to him. "I didn't learn to sail to please Dad. I didn't want to be a wimp."

He sat up, too, and kissed her neck. "Hurricane Ariel, you couldn't be a wimp if you tried."

"Then why are we talking about this?" Jeff heard a tremor in her voice. "It happened a long time ago."

He stroked her hair. "I think you're still trying to please your dad."

"That's crazy."

Jeff was pretty sure it wasn't crazy. "I just want you to be happy—for yourself."

She twisted around to look at him, her eyes wide. "I am happy here with you."

He heard the plea and answered it, pulling her into his arms and holding her tightly.

"Make love with me, Jeff. I need you again."

He kissed her, then took her quickly. *Speed*, he thought. She needed speed and heat and wildness to escape whatever demons his questions had called forth. And he gave them to her, racing with her, driving her... until she lay quiescent in his arms, the soft smile on her lips telling him he'd erased whatever troubled her, at least for tonight.

Still, he had an uneasy feeling that some piece of the puzzle of Ariel Foster was still missing.

12

"THREE MEMBERS OF St. Elizabeth's Hospital's board of trustees were indicted today for diverting hospital funds for their own profit." Hal told the story simply. There was no hoopla, no one camped on the trustees' lawns. The *Mariner* commended Channel 4 on the op-ed page. Even Jeff admitted the coverage was fair.

As August drew to a close, the station's ratings edged upward. Ariel dashed off faxes to her brothers to advise them she was hot on their tails. Then, remembering the way Jeff had looked at her when she'd first worn the black nightie, she rewarded herself with some sexy underwear—a reckless extravagance, since he'd just tear it off her.

On September first, Wendy Norris joined the staff as evening coanchor and was an immediate success. She was less successful with Steve, Ariel noted, because Kara was keeping him extremely busy. Steve had never looked so happy.

Ariel was happy, too. Happier than she'd ever been. On the other hand, though she was normally the most optimistic of persons, she didn't allow herself to think too much about her future with Jeff. Maybe it was superstition, but she didn't want to count her chickens before they hatched.

Besides, something nagged at her. Jeff had begun to trust her since he'd seen how she handled the hospital situation, and their relationship had reached a new plane. What would he think if he found out about the family contest? He'd be furious, but why would he ever have to know? If she won—*when* she won—she could simply tell him she'd been transferred to Houston.

And leave him? The specter of Keith and her broken engagement reared its ugly head. But Keith had had a business in Fort Worth. The weather was everywhere, wasn't it? Maybe Jeff could transfer to Houston, too. Somehow they would work things out. Meanwhile they were enjoying one another...and the summer had passed without even the hint of a hurricane.

But on September fifth, a tropical storm named Chester skittered westward across the Gulf of Mexico. "Will it hit Corpus?" Ariel asked nervously on Friday evening.

"We can't be a hundred percent certain, but it looks like it'll make landfall somewhere in Mexico," Jeff replied. "We shouldn't have to change our picnic plans for tomorrow. We may get some showers but not until later in the day."

Noon the next day found them at the small park in Ariel's neighborhood. The day was hot and humid, not unlike the Fourth of July, the first day they'd picnicked together. Jeff turned his boom box to KCOR-FM, and after sharing a lunch of chicken salad and fruit at one of the old wooden picnic tables beneath the trees, they spread a blanket on the ground and lay side by side, enjoying the afternoon.

Sea gulls soared overhead, then dipped and dived, calling out like boisterous children. In the trees nearby, a flock of sparrows congregated, twittering and chirping as if they were sharing the latest gossip. White clouds scudded across the sky directly above them, but to the south they could see gray. The air held the scent of rain.

Ariel watched Jeff as he leaned back on one elbow—one *sexy* elbow. God, she was crazy about him. She loved talking to him, spending time with him, doing anything from playing tennis to arguing about the state of the world to making love.

"This is nice." He took a deep breath. "Quiet."

"Aren't you enjoying your notoriety, just a little?"

"A little." He grinned at her. "The Miss Corpus Christi Pageant Committee called and asked me to judge next year."

"Oh?" She couldn't help it if she sounded huffy. The Miss Corpus Christi Pageant, indeed.

"I guess I should think about it."

"*Oh?*" Getting used to the limelight was one thing. Ogling a bunch of half-naked beauties was something else.

Jeff plucked a blade of grass and fingered it lazily. "I turned them down."

"Oh!"

He stretched his legs and contemplated his tennis shoes. "Of course, I could still change my mind with the right incentive. Maybe if they hook me up with Miss Congeniality . . ."

"Don't even think it," Ariel ordered. "You know," she added, "you're coming out of your shell."

He sighed. "Yeah, but if I could get the women off my tail, I'd be happier. Someone sent me a bra yesterday."

"You must have quite a lingerie collection by now," Ariel said. "What have you done with it?"

"Donated it to the Salvation Army."

"But being a celebrity has advantages, don't you think?"

Jeff considered her question. Finally he answered, "I have the chance to contribute something to the city, and that's good. I'm getting used to being recognized, but I'll never be as comfortable in the spotlight as you are. You seem to thrive on it." He brushed a finger along her cheek, then said, "We're different in so many ways, I often ask myself how we get along."

"Opposites attract."

Jeff groaned. "Ouch. Why didn't I see that coming?"

"Seriously, Jeff. I think it *is* the differences that excite us. We're learning to enjoy each other's tastes and that's broadened both our lives. That walk we took on Sunday, along the sand dunes on Padre Island, just the two of us—it wasn't something I would have thought of."

"You'd have invited fifty people along and organized a volleyball tournament."

"Yes, but the point is, I loved it. I'm seeing the beauty in quiet, something I never did before."

"I'm glad."

She beamed at him and turned on her stomach, totally relaxed, staring lazily at the grass. Her eyes lit on a spider energetically spinning its web. She smiled and began to recite.

"'The Spider as an Artist
Has never been employed—
Though his surpassing merit
Is freely certified

By every Broom and Bridget
Throughout a Christian Land—
Neglected Son of Genius
I take thee by the Hand—'

Emily Dickinson," she added.

Jeff turned on his side to watch the industrious spider. "Weather lore says that when humidity is high and air pressure drops, spiders work harder and build larger nets. This one seems pretty busy. Look at the sky." The gray clouds, which had been far to the south earlier, seemed nearer now. "When the clouds get closer, she'll pull the web down," he continued, "so the bugs she caught won't get washed away by the rain."

"Sounds sensible."

"Indoor spiders work like crazy before and during a storm and take a rest when the weather starts to clear."

"So that's how you scientist types make your forecasts," Ariel teased. "You sit around watching spiders."

"They're pretty accurate predictors," Jeff said. "There's a story about a French general—I don't recall his name— who'd been tossed into prison for losing a battle in rainy weather during the Franco-Prussian War. He didn't have anything better to do, so he watched the spiders spinning webs in the corners of his cell. One day he noticed that they'd stopped, and he remembered the proverb that said when spiders quit expanding their webs, the weather will clear. So he convinced his commander to let him out, launched another battle against the Prussians in more favorable weather, and won."

"And was proclaimed a hero," Ariel finished.

"Probably," he agreed.

With a languid sigh, Ariel rolled onto her back. "It's peaceful out here. Makes me sleepy."

"Why don't you take a nap?" he suggested. "You've been going like gangbusters all week. You deserve it." He turned off the radio.

"Mmm." She shut her eyes and dozed off.

When she awoke, the sky had darkened. The clouds were heavy now, blotting out the sun. In the grass beside her, the little spider was working feverishly at taking down her web. "A storm," Ariel murmured, realizing the breeze had picked up, too. In fact, it was no longer a breeze but a wind. "Do you think the hurricane's coming this way?"

"Tropical storm," Jeff corrected. "The winds aren't strong enough for a hurricane. It's probably still south of here, but we're getting the fringes."

"Shouldn't we go?" she asked uneasily, sitting up.

Jeff checked the sky with an expert's eye. "We have a while before we have to worry about rain." He reached for the radio and flipped through stations. "Let's see what's happening."

"Tropical Storm Chester, with winds of forty-seven miles an hour gusting to sixty, is presently located approximately thirty miles offshore, south of Matamoros, Mexico, and moving at twelve miles per hour. Chester is expected to make landfall this evening between seven and ten. Residents in the area should take proper precautions. A storm watch is in effect for areas along the south Texas coast from Corpus Christi to Brownsville."

Jeff grimaced. "'Proper precautions' is pretty vague. Let's hope the residents down there know what that means."

"Maybe next year we can offer tapes of your shows so they will. We can even have them translated into Spanish." Funny, she was thinking about next year. But by then she planned to be in Houston. Didn't she?

A sudden gust slapped her cheeks. Grass rippled in the wind like an ocean of green. Ariel looked for the spider. She was gone. "Jeff, I think we should pack up." Nervously, she searched for the sunglasses she'd removed before she'd fallen asleep. She found them at the edge of the blanket and tossed them into her purse. She glanced at the sky. It seemed even darker now. In the distance, thunder rolled. "My shoes," she muttered. "Where'd they go? I know I—" Absorbed in the radio, Jeff paid no attention. Ariel finally retrieved a shoe from under the blanket, tried to put it on, and struggled with the strap. "Damn! Why do things go wrong when you're in a rush?"

Jeff leaned back and stretched. "We don't have to hurry."

"I . . . I don't want to get wet."

"You won't," he said with annoying unconcern. "But since you're so anxious to go, we'll pack up." He rose and picked up their hamper and the radio.

Ariel found her other shoe, stood up on one foot, hopped, and yanked the shoe over her bare foot.

Jeff gave her an amused smile. "Relax, honey. You won't ruin your hairdo, I promise."

"Come off it, McBride. Meteorology isn't an exact science." Lightning split the sky. "See!" She grabbed the blanket without bothering to fold it and started for the car. An earsplitting clap of thunder sounded directly overhead. Ariel gasped and bolted for the parking lot, forgetting she carried the blanket. She tripped on the edge of the cloth and tumbled onto the grass.

Winded, she sprawled there, heart pounding, eyes shut. Instantly, Jeff was beside her. "Are you okay?"

Tears sprang to her eyes. "No, I mean, yes. I don't know."

He put his arms around her. "Honey, what's wrong?"

"Nothing," Ariel muttered. "I just want to—" The wind caught her words and spun them away. Thunder crashed. She huddled closer to Jeff, shivering.

He tightened his arms about her. "You're scared to death."

Humiliated by her behavior, by her tears, but powerless to control them, Ariel nodded. "The thunder. . ."

"Okay, baby, let's get you home." He stood and pulled her to her feet. "Come on."

Feeling about six years old, Ariel trotted along beside him. She hated herself, hated her fear. Most of all, she hated displaying her weakness in front of Jeff. *You think you're a big shot*, she castigated herself silently. *But no, you're a wimp.* She'd have to explain, she decided, as they got into the car.

Jeff pulled out of the parking lot, then drove with one hand, the other holding Ariel's against his thigh. Calmer now in the shelter of the car, she took a breath. "I guess you think it's silly to get so frightened," she ventured. That's what her brother Daniel had thought more than once when she'd cowered in her room with her hands over her ears during an electrical storm.

"I think you're afraid of thunderstorms, and you must have a reason."

"It started when I was around five," she said. "Chad and Daniel and I were playing hide-and-seek. My parents were having some repairs done on the house. One of the workmen left the attic stairs down, and I decided to hide up there. It was late in the afternoon, and while I was hiding, he put the stairs back up and left. When I realized what had happened, I thought it was funny. I could hear Chad walking around in the hallway below, hunting for me in the closets, but I kept quiet. I figured I'd tap on the ceiling and scare him to death. Then he went off to look somewhere else, and it wasn't so funny anymore."

"What happened?"

"It started to rain, one of those storms that happens in a flash." Suddenly she was back in that dark, musty attic with rain pounding on the roof. "There was hail," she said, hearing it again like a hundred rifle shots clattering above her head. "And thunder. Awful thunder. It was dark as midnight. I started thinking about rats and bats— vampire bats. I was afraid lightning would strike the roof, that thunder would explode all around me.

"Didn't you try to get out?"

"Of course. I pushed on the door but I couldn't open it. Then I screamed and pounded on the ceiling, but the boys must've gone downstairs. No one heard me. I was trapped, all alone up there." She shivered. "The walls started closing in around me."

Jeff squeezed her hand. "Poor kid."

"After a while, I couldn't breathe. I imagined some monster had sucked up all the air. I don't know if I hy- perventilated or what, but I must have passed out be- cause the next thing I knew, the storm had passed and everything was quiet. I heard someone calling my name—not Chad or Daniel, but my father. I had the strangest feeling, as if I were half-awake, half in a night- mare. I heard the voices downstairs, but I couldn't call out. I must have cried my voice away. Finally, I heard someone coming down the hall, and I banged on the at- tic floor. Dad came up and got me. I remember how re- lieved I was to see him, how glad I was to see daylight and how scared and white my brothers' faces were when Dad carried me down into the hall. I've been terrified of storms ever since," she finished. "Ridiculous, huh?"

"Reasonable," Jeff corrected. "But what does your fa- ther think about your fears?"

"I never told him." He nodded as if he'd expected that, and Ariel scowled. "Why do you always bring up my fa- ther?"

"Because I think you live your life to please him."

"That's ridiculous."

"Is it? You're always comparing ratings with your brothers. Your fax machine goes night and day."

Ariel didn't answer. Instead, she turned and looked out the window. If Jeff knew what she was really competing for, what would he think?

As Jeff turned the corner by his apartment building, the first drops of rain splattered against the car windows. Inside, in the elevator, he said, "Phobias can be treated, you know. Have you ever considered therapy?"

She shook her head, relieved he'd abandoned the topic of her father. "Once a storm's over, I forget about it. Until the next one."

When they stepped into Jeff's living room, they found Blizzard crouched under the coffee table. "He doesn't like storms, either," Jeff explained. "The minute the barometric pressure drops, he heads for cover." He bent down and put out a hand to the cat. Blizzard shrank back. "The pressure must be way down."

"Now I know your secret. You rely on cats, not spiders." Thunder crashed again. She jumped and moved closer to Jeff.

"You need to learn to associate thunder with relaxation," he said. "Want to try it?"

His look dared her to say no. Well, she'd never been one to back away from a challenge. Martin Foster had seen to that. "Sure."

"Come into the bedroom."

She followed him, and watched dubiously as he went to the window and threw the drapes wide open. Ariel refused to let herself cringe, even though rain pounded against the glass like a monster trying to break in.

"Come here."

Slowly, she walked toward him. He drew her into his arms and kissed her. Softly, gently. "Relax," he murmured, and stroked her hair. "Close your eyes. Think of a country lane on a quiet afternoon."

"Mmm." She saw the winding lane, the green, clover-scented grass, a cow grazing behind an old wooden fence.

Jeff undid her blouse, slipped it from her shoulders. He kneaded the taut muscles in her neck, loosening them. In the field she saw wildflowers, white and purple, nodding in a gentle breeze. Eyes still closed, half dreaming, she felt Jeff unfasten her bra, slip her shorts and panties down. She stepped out of them, wriggled out of her sandals. "Open your eyes," he whispered.

The rain still slammed against the window, but Jeff stood between her and the storm. He lifted her into his arms, then laid her on the bed. "Be right back."

She rolled onto her stomach, shut her eyes again and imagined the field of flowers, the black-and-white cow, a farmhouse in the distance. In a few minutes, she felt the bed sink and opened her eyes to see Jeff, stripped down to his shorts, with a bottle in his hand. "I'm going to give you a massage," he said. "Just relax and look out the window."

She stared at the rain. The sound lulled her now as Jeff spread lotion over her shoulders and back. Then thunder sounded, and she tensed, her hands balling into fists.

"Shh, it's okay, it's okay." His voice was so calm, his touch was so soothing. Her hands relaxed, her muscles slackened and she floated, while his hands worked their magic along her spine. Her breathing deepened as she lay in a gray, rainy world—in the midst of the storm, but safe.

"Turn over."

He smoothed lotion over her skin, stroking her breasts, her stomach, her thighs. The sound of the rain was hypnotic. She sighed, feeling more relaxed than she'd ever been; as if she could lie here forever, drowsy and serene. But gradually, she became aware of other sensations, tingling sensations as light fingers traced her hipbones, grazed the sides of her breasts. "Jeff." She sighed, looking up at him. His eyes were dark, intense. She lifted her arms. "Make love with me."

He pulled off his briefs and knelt over her. Slipping into her easily, he gently made love to her.

When it was over and they lay close, Ariel let out a soft breath. Behind Jeff, she could see the rain drumming at the window. She could still hear thunder in the distance, but she was no longer afraid. Years later, whenever she heard thunder she'd think of this afternoon, remember Jeff's tender caresses. Would he be just a memory, too? No! She was in love with him. She wanted them to be together always. Somehow she'd have to make that happen.

She kissed his cheek. "I don't think I'll ever feel quite the same about a thunderstorm."

"Neither will I."

THE FOLLOWING WEEK, the National Hurricane Service began tracking a tropical depression. Four days later, it was upgraded to a tropical storm and given the name Daphne. Another forty-eight hours, and Daphne grew into a full-fledged hurricane.

Jeff studied the course of the storm with intense interest; Ariel shuddered at the thought of it. Maybe she could handle thunder better now, but a hurricane was something else. Theoretically, hurricanes were a fascinating subject, and of course, they'd brought Jeff and her together, but the idea of one of those monster storms striking Corpus Christi scared her to death.

Daphne didn't head toward Texas; instead she flirted with the East Coast, dancing along past the Carolinas, the middle Atlantic states and even New England. Like a shy lover, she came closer, then backed away. Finally, she stalled offshore, and except for enduring prodigious amounts of rainfall, the Atlantic coast was unscathed.

As coastal residents breathed sighs of relief over Daphne's demise, another tropical depression loomed behind her.

"This one's developing quickly," Jeff observed. On his spot that evening, he advised Corpus Christians to keep abreast of weather advisories. The remainder of September, he added, might prove to be a turbulent month.

By the next morning, the depression had been upgraded to a tropical storm and named Ethan.

After discussing the situation with Steve, Ariel called Jeff and asked him to meet in her office that evening. "I want to have a business conversation," she explained.

"And you don't believe in mixing business with pleasure." His voice was warm with laughter.

"In this case, no."

Later, when he sat across the desk from her, he said, "You sounded serious. Is something wrong?"

"No, but with another storm out there, we should increase our coverage to daily thirty-second inserts after the weather report at six and ten in the evening. I'd like you to do them."

She waited anxiously for Jeff's response. She'd taken the precaution of inserting a new affirmation into her routine for that day: "I easily win agreement for adding to Channel 4's hurricane coverage."

"Might as well," he said amiably, and Ariel let out a breath. "I'm here every evening anyway." He stretched his hands in front of him and frowned at them. "But can we skip the makeup? It's already soaked through my pores. I'm turning orange."

Ariel laughed. "It's the light in here. We've been through this before, Jeff. Without makeup, you'll look like the Hurricane Ghost."

"Better that than the Hurricane Hunk," he muttered. "Okay, I give up, but tell Lynn I only need a sixth of the makeup I use for a three-minute spot."

"Deal," Ariel said. "We'll start Monday. I'll tell Kara."

The producer was pleased, Steve was pleased; Perry Weston was not. Kara reported that when she told him the plan, he objected strongly. "He said we were cutting coverage of important local weather news to focus on a piddly storm thousands of miles away."

"Piddly? Did he really say that?"

"Yep. It's hard to imagine a tropical storm being piddly."

"And if it comes this way," Ariel added, "it *will* be local news."

"I tried my best to convince him coverage was an important part of our hurricane-awareness program. I ended up saying the decision had been made."

"And?"

"He muttered something and stomped out."

Ariel sighed. "I'd better talk to Perry myself."

She cornered him in the hall after the six o'clock news that evening. "I'd like to talk with you," she said.

"What about?"

How typically Perry, she thought. He knew darn well what about. Hoping to handle the situation diplomatically, she said, "I realize you aren't happy with Dr. McBride coming on, and I thought we could discuss it."

Perry stared at her, his face expressionless. "What's to discuss?"

"I wanted to make it clear this is a short-term measure while this hurricane is building."

"What hurricane?" Perry said. "There is no hurricane."

Ariel knew he was being deliberately obtuse. She wanted to kick him. "Tropical storm," she amended.

"Is that it?"

"Yes."

"Then I see no need to talk anymore." He lumbered off.

Later, she reported the conversation to Steve and added, "Perry drives me nuts. I'd like to ship him off to Chad."

"I don't think Chad would accept. Perry'd come flying back from San Antonio faster than the speed of sound."

"Not my brother Chad. I mean Chad, the country. As in Africa."

"Nice idea," Steve agreed. "But then, who'd do the noon and evening weather reports?"

"Good point." Ariel sighed. "If we lose Perry now, we'll be in a real bind." Even thinking about it made her shudder. "I guess we'll have to do our best to keep Old Stone Face happy until I can look around for someone to take his place."

"Maybe you're overreacting," Steve said. "Perry did say there was no need to talk."

"But is that good or bad?" Somehow Ariel didn't feel the problem with Perry had been resolved.

It hadn't.

Monday evening when Jeff came on the set, Perry glared at him with open animosity. When Jeff tried to catch up with him after the news, Perry deliberately ignored the overture and stalked out of the building.

The following morning when Ariel arrived at the station, Perry was waiting for her. "I want to talk to you."

"Come in." He marched into her office and sat down heavily in the chair across from her. "What's on your mind?" she asked.

"The blowhard."

Ariel frowned. *Blow hard? Hard blow?* "The storm?"

Perry looked at her as if she'd lost her mind. "The meteorologist." He snorted. "He may know about hurricanes, but he doesn't know beans about television weather."

Ariel held her tongue, though she was tempted to ask if television weather was somehow different from real weather.

Perry didn't want a reply anyway. "I've been with this station for seventeen years," he grumbled. "Now *you* waltz in and try to change things. Bringing in some slick talker you can write up in the society columns—"

"He's—"

Perry didn't wait for her to continue. "I've put up with all of it—newfangled graphics and weather charts, a half-grown girl producing the news, female anchors in skirts up to their armpits—but this...*this*—" His voice cracked "—cutting into my time is the last straw. You want this station to be an MTV clone? Fine. Do it without me." He pulled a paper from his pocket and tossed it onto the desk. "I quit."

13

ARIEL STARED AT HIM in shock. She'd anticipated a tantrum; she hadn't expected Perry to resign. "You . . . you can't," she sputtered.

Perry got to his feet. "Watch me. Tomorrow's my last day."

She shot out of her chair. "We have a contract. You can't walk out."

"Sue me," he said over his shoulder, then opened the door and stomped out.

Ariel gazed after him for a long moment, before she slumped down in her chair and picked up the phone. "Steve, can you come in here a minute? We have a problem."

While she waited for Steve, Ariel reminded herself that this wasn't the first crisis she'd faced. She remembered the time in Beaumont when Hector—a live goat and a newcomer on the children's show she produced—had eaten half the set. And the evening her sportscaster in Fort Worth had come in dead drunk and announced that the Dallas Cowboys had been sold to owners from Mexico City and would thenceforth be called the Chihuahuas...and had practically started a riot among football fans. She'd weathered these and other less colorful disasters. Surely she could weather the weather.

Steve interrupted her thoughts. "What's the problem?"

"Perry quit."

"So? Isn't that what we've been hoping for?"

"You don't understand." She heard her voice crack and tried to calm down. "He didn't give notice. After tomorrow he's outta here."

"Oh, Lord." Steve sank onto a chair. "I don't believe it."

"Believe it." She shoved Perry's letter across the desk.

Steve scanned it, then muttered, "I didn't think he had the guts." He tossed the paper aside. "What are our options?"

"Well, we can go to Plan A ... or Plan A."

"In other words, we have no options," Steve said.

"Right. We'll have to use Charles." Charles Henke, the morning weathercaster, had been with the station for six months.

"Well," Steve said, "the good news is he comes across well. Viewers like him. I think he has the makings of a top-notch broadcaster."

"Makings," Ariel emphasized. "That's the bad news. He's inexperienced. And the worst news is—"

"He's not a meteorologist," they chorused.

"Right," Ariel continued. "As you said, he has potential, *but*—"

"But he's no Jeff McBride," Steve finished.

Ariel sighed. "Sad but true. And he'd have to go on right before Jeff every evening because of those thirty-second inserts. *And* another hurricane's out there. Well, we can't do anything about that ... unless ... *unless* ..."

"Uh-oh. I can see the wheels turning," Steve said. "And I can guess what you're coming up with."

"Yeah." She leaned forward excitedly. "Why don't we ask *Jeff* to do the weather at noon, six and ten? People love him, and who knows more about storms? Perfect solution. Let's do it."

"Aren't you forgetting one small detail?" Steve asked. "He has another job."

"A minor detail."

"He *likes* his other job."

Ariel waved a hand dismissively. "I'll ask him tonight."

"Ask away," Steve said. "I hate to rain on your parade, Ariel, but I think he'll say no."

"No."

"But, Jeff—"

"*No!* That's N-o. Absolutely, positively, definitely, *no!*" He folded his arms across his chest.

"Jeff, be reasonable."

"No, you be reasonable." He leaned toward her, staring her down—and staring Ariel Foster down wasn't easy. "I do not work in television. I don't *want* to work in television. I'm doing these—whatever you call them—segments, as a community service, not as a career move."

"You said yourself September would be a turbulent month. The station needs you. The *city* needs you," she said firmly.

Oh, God! "Don't try to lay another guilt trip on me." Damn, he should have known when she called to set up another appointment in her office that she was up to something. "Look," he said, "I'm sorry about your problems with Perry, but I'm not your solution. You have another weatherman, don't you? Use him."

"He doesn't have the knowledge you do."

Jeff shook his head again. "He'll have to read the reports from the Hurricane Center. He can read, can't he?"

Ariel ignored the sarcasm. "What's the status of Ethan?"

Oh, she was clever. "The storm's been upgraded to hurricane. It's two hundred miles east of Hispaniola."

There was a long silence. But Jeff could almost hear her thoughts: *Nobody in Corpus knows more about hurricanes than you.*

"I have a job, remember?" he reminded her. "I can't walk out on my commitment."

"We could talk to your boss."

"And he'd say no."

"You can't be sure until you ask."

Damn, she was wasted here. She should be negotiating for the State Department. "I don't *want* to ask."

"*I'll ask*," she offered. "I'll explain this is just until Ethan is out of the way."

"Are you sure of that?"

She nodded vigorously.

"Will you put it in black and white?"

"In blood if you want," she said, moving in for the kill.

He spread his hands. Ariel picked up the phone. Within minutes, she had charmed Wayne, and the traitor had said yes. Ariel handed Jeff the phone, and Wayne said, "The South Texas contract is under control. Nothing new in the works right now. You can take a leave of absence for a month. No problem."

"You see?" Ariel grinned when he hung up. "That worked out just fine."

Feeling as if he'd been run over by a steamroller, Jeff said, "Just one thing."

"What?"

"You owe me for this."

"I know, Jeff," she said solemnly. "Anything you want."

"Good. I'll take my first payment as soon as we get home. In bed."

DOING THE WEATHER AT twelve, six and ten was a snap, Jeff concluded. A lot easier to read the reports from the National Hurricane Center than to put them together as he'd done when he worked there. He had plenty of time to work out the final details of his upcoming research project with Florida State as well as to broadcast the weather reports. And he *was* being of service to the city. That was the bottom line.

There were drawbacks, too, though. TV weather reporting wasn't challenging. Jeff couldn't understand why someone would consider making a career of it. Despite that, Jeff enjoyed the excitement and turmoil of the TV station. Something was always happening. You never knew until the last minute what news stories would run. His respect for Kara and the news team increased a hundred percent as he watched them work.

He continued following the progress of Hurricane Ethan. The storm wandered about the Atlantic haphazardly for a couple of days, then seemed to make a decision. Picking up speed, it again began moving toward Hispaniola.

Friday morning Jeff faced the camera. "Last night at eleven-forty Hurricane Ethan struck the island of Hispaniola with sustained winds of 115 miles an hour, cutting a wide swath from east to west and ravaging both the Dominican Republic and Haiti, the two countries that share the island. This tape just in." The film showed raging winds, uprooted trees, wooden huts reduced to piles of kindling, a luxury hotel with gaping holes where plate-glass windows had been and a pool filled with debris.

"Eleven people were killed and several hundred injured. As Ethan leaves Hispaniola gasping in its wake, the Caribbean waits nervously to see what Ethan may do next. Stay tuned for periodic updates on Ethan from the National Hurricane Center in Florida."

Ariel shuddered when Jeff came into her office later. "Ethan's a scary storm. Do you think it's likely to intensify now that it's past Hispaniola?"

"Very likely," Jeff said. "Once it's out to sea, it can gain strength again."

By late that afternoon, Ethan had headed into the Caribbean. There, fueled by warm air and moisture, it grew larger, and, like a giant hunting for quarry, began a march across the water.

Jeff kept in touch with the National Hurricane Center in Miami as Ethan roared across the western tip of Cuba and swung into the Gulf of Mexico. There, as if temporarily sated, it paused, but Jeff was certain the respite was brief. Soon Ethan would move again.

But no one seemed concerned about the storm.

With the exception of the members of the Emergency Planning Commission, most residents of Corpus Christi paid no mind to the behemoth lurking in the Gulf. Ethan was too far away.

"Prob'ly gonna hit Mississippi," the guy filling his pickup at the pump next to Jeff remarked. "Ain't that many of them storms ever come this way."

"This could be the one that does. It's headed in this direction," Jeff told him.

"It'll turn."

"I don't think so," Jeff said. "I'm a meteorologist."

The man aimed a stream of chewing tobacco at the pavement. "I don't hold with that scientific bunk. My bones tell me that storm's gonna hit way off." He topped off his tank and ambled over to the window to pay for his gas.

As Ethan edged west, Jeff's bones told him the opposite. He saw no indication that the storm was taking a northward turn toward Mississippi.

But no one listened. The prospects of the Ball High football team, the escalating price of beef, the latest scandals in Washington and Austin were the hot topics of conversation around town. As the weekend began, Corpus Christians ignored the storm and went blithely on with their plans. And Channel 12, Ariel's competitor, didn't help matters. Jeff had heard that the other station was downplaying the hurricane, but he wanted to see for himself. He taped the Saturday-evening weathercast, and when he and Ariel got home, he turned it on.

Nancy Barker, the Channel 12 weatherperson, smiled into the camera, displaying a set of perfect teeth. She read the Sunday forecast in a cheery voice. She looked like a Dallas Cowboys cheerleader. At any minute, Jeff expected her to grab a pom-pom and wave it.

"A super day tomorrow," she chirped. "Clear, hot, and humid." Then she gestured to the weather map with scarlet-tipped fingers. "And now for an update on Hurricane Ethan. As you can see, the storm is still approximately 370 miles east of Corpus Christi and moving slowly west-northwest at eleven miles an hour. Probability that the eye will pass over Corpus Christi is still low, according to the National Hurricane Center in Miami. So don't cancel those Sunday picnics or trips to the beach. Before we know it, cool weather will be here. For now, enjoy."

The news anchor smiled at Ms. Barker as the camera pulled back for a view of the anchor desk. "Good to hear Ethan's not a threat at this time. What *should* people be doing, Nancy?"

She gave him a perky cheerleader smile. "I'm guh-lad you asked, Tom. Take sensible precautions—be sure you have a flashlight and batteries handy, and bottled water—but no need to panic."

Jeff grimaced. "Channel 12 should have their heads examined. They're downplaying a potentially dangerous storm, and after what happened with the last storm two years ago, people are listening to them."

"I was in Fort Worth then," Ariel reminded him.

"I know. Your station got the city all worked up about Hurricane Clark, had people ready to evacuate, and then the storm hit Louisiana."

"But this is a different storm."

"Of course, but when folks think you've cried wolf once, they're not apt to believe you the next time. Even when they should."

"You think they should, don't you?" Ariel asked.

"I'm an old Boy Scout. I believe in being prepared."

She put her hand over her heart. "Heavens! A cliché."

"Rubs off." He switched off the TV and VCR. "At least Mayor Cameron is taking a sensible view. He's got everyone on alert—the Red Cross, the police department, fire department, you name it."

"So we're ready."

"Officially. Now let's hope the man on the street pays attention."

SUNDAY MORNING ARIEL stepped onto Jeff's balcony and took a breath of balmy air. The day was beautiful, with clear blue skies and a light breeze. "Maybe Nancy Barker knew what she was talking about," Ariel said hopefully. This once, she hoped her competitor was right.

Jeff followed her out and shook his head. "The weather surrounding a hurricane system is often unusually nice."

Ariel glanced over her shoulder into the living room where the cat snoozed, precisely in the center of a square of sunlight. "Blizzard doesn't seem worried."

"Pressure hasn't dropped yet." Jeff put his arm around Ariel's shoulders. "Come on. Let's go over to the station. I want to check the latest advisory, see how much closer the storm is."

Ariel shivered. She didn't want to go. She didn't want to know about the storm. Jeff might have calmed her fears about thunderstorms, but hurricanes were in a class by themselves. "Why don't you drop me off at home? I need to . . . do my laundry."

Jeff looked at her quizzically but didn't comment.

When they reached her town house, she hurried to the door, stopping to pick up the Sunday paper. Ethan hadn't even made the front page. *Good.* But on the inside pages were new pictures of the havoc the hurricane had wreaked on Hispaniola and Cuba. Awful pictures. Ariel tossed the newspaper aside.

Not wanting Jeff to catch her in a lie, she began tossing clothes into the washer. When she turned it on, she left the top up and peered, fascinated, at the churning water pulling the clothing down, whirling it around— like a hurricane. Damn, she couldn't escape Ethan even in the laundry room.

Ariel plodded back into the kitchen, opened her pantry and surveyed the shelves. Did she have adequate supplies to last through a storm? "What did Jeff say you need?" she muttered to herself, wishing she'd paid more attention to what he said on TV than how he looked. Of course, she didn't intend to stay here during a storm. But what if it hit at night? What if it blew off the roof? Then she wouldn't need to worry about food, would she?

Anyway, if the storm did strike during the night, she wouldn't be alone. Jeff would be here—or would he? No, he'd be at the station, broadcasting. And, damn it, so would she. No way was she going to get stranded here. Not that she couldn't manage on her own, but the station was safer.

The doorbell rang, and she let Jeff in. He didn't wait for her to ask for news. "Ethan's slowed, but still heading in this direction. We're under a hurricane watch now."

Ariel swallowed. "What should we do?"

"I think we'd better go by the hardware store and pick up some plywood."

"Plywood? But we don't need to board up yet, not with the storm still far away."

"We're just going to buy it. If we wait until Ethan's close, everyone will be sold out."

Ariel didn't want to buy plywood. Plywood meant the storm was real—not just pictures in the paper or reports on television—but, in the face of Jeff's logic, she couldn't think of an excuse. At the hardware store, she lagged behind Jeff, stopping to look at a display of wrenches, letting a handful of two-inch nails sift through her fingers, examining a tool chest. "Going in for carpentry?" Jeff inquired, and she shrugged.

On the way back to her town house, she said crossly, "The store wasn't busy. Nobody else was buying plywood."

"No one else is sleeping with a meteorologist."

Her next-door neighbor, a thirty-something fellow whom she knew only slightly, pulled up just after they did. "What's going on?" he asked, stopping to gawk as Jeff lugged the plywood out of his car. "You remodeling?"

"Getting ready for Ethan," Jeff said without turning.

"You know, the hurricane," Ariel added.

Her neighbor guffawed. "Hell, those things never end up here. You two been listening to some doomsayer?"

Jeff stopped halfway to the door. "I'm the doomsayer." He raised his eyes and pointed east. "See those clouds fanning out on the horizon?"

"Those little wisps," the fellow said, shading his eyes. "Can't hardly see them."

"You'll see more of them. The Spanish used to call them *rabos de gallo*, rooster tails. They're cirrus clouds, and they're a sign of an approaching storm."

"Sounds like a lot of hooey to me."

Ariel wished it sounded that way to her.

14

THE NEXT DAY THE CLOUDS were still far to the east, but they were denser.

The storm had not turned, and it was nearer. At eight in the morning, it was 207 miles east-southeast of Corpus and stealing closer. As it prowled the Gulf, offshore oil rigs were abandoned, a small-craft advisory was announced, and the mayor authorized the Emergency Planning Commission to finalize preparations.

Jeff and Debra shot their spot early. The camera filmed her securing the house and packing to leave for the Red Cross center.

"Just in case?" she asked when they finished.

"I think there's a good chance you'll have to go. See how cloudy the sky is, and see that halo around the sun? That's not a good sign."

Debra paled. "All summer we've been talkin' about storms, but it was like playacting. It didn't seem real."

"It's real now."

She glanced at her home. "I hate the thought of leaving." Her voice shook. "The house might not be here when we get back."

Jeff put his arm around her. "I know. But you *will* go."

"Sure."

"Keep your TV on. We'll broadcast the latest advisories the minute they come in. And when I say to leave, do it."

"Okay. I can help out at the center when we go. I guess I know about as much about hurricanes as anybody."

"That's the spirit," he said, squeezing her hand. "After the storm's over, we'll tape you coming back home."

"Okay. Jeff," she added as he started to walk away, "you've been great this summer. If that storm hits and we survive—if *anyone* survives—it'll be because of you."

"Thanks," he said and went back to the van where the cameraman waited. "Drop me back at the station, would you? Then I'd like you to film the beach. Show the tide rising. Get some shots of the sky."

As he entered the station, he met Ariel coming down the hall, a weekend case in her hand. "Where are you going?"

"San Antonio. Don't you remember? I'm speaking at a conference tomorrow morning."

He'd forgotten. He grabbed her arm before she could walk away. "I don't think you should go."

She jerked it back. "I have to."

Two secretaries walked by, glancing at them with interest. "Let's go in your office for a minute," he said.

Inside, he closed the door. "Ariel—"

"Jeff, San Antonio is 150 miles inland. The storm's hardly going to do any damage there."

"That's not what I'm worried about. I don't like the idea of you being on the road in the middle of nowhere alone. You could be on your way back here when Ethan hits."

For a moment, she looked frightened. "Is it closer?"

"Uh-huh. It's stalled again, but it could start to move any moment."

She glanced nervously out the window. "Maybe I should go home first and board up."

For a moment, he considered telling her yes. That would keep her here longer, and maybe she'd cancel the trip after all. Or she'd start off at night, and he didn't want her on the road after dark, storm or no storm. "I'll see that it's taken care of. Give me an extra key."

"Thanks." Ariel set down her bag, handed him the key, then put her arms around him. "Jeff, nobody is more afraid of storms than I am. If Ethan gets too close, I'll stay in San Antonio. I'll be at Chad's."

He took her face between his hands, the face he couldn't live without. "Promise me."

"I promise."

"Where's the conference?" he asked.

"The Marriott."

"Do you have your car phone?"

"Yes, Dad."

He pulled her close and kissed her hard. If anything happened to her— He couldn't bear to think of it. "Be careful."

"I will. See you tomorrow. I'll be back by eleven-thirty." She picked up her bag and strode out of the office.

Jeff took a step after her as the door closed behind her. Damn it, he shouldn't let her go. But Ariel was no easier to control than Ethan. Like the storm, she'd go her own way in her own time. He sighed, called the handyman who occasionally worked for him and got a promise that he'd put plywood over Ariel's windows in the evening. They made arrangements to meet, then Jeff went to choose film clips of Ethan's destruction in Haiti and Cuba to add to his weather report. Perhaps if people saw again the havoc wreaked on the islands, they'd pay attention now that the storm was closer to home.

While he was working, one of the secretaries called him to the phone.

"Dr. McBride, this is Opal Hayes."

Jeff frowned. His housekeeper wasn't due to come in again until Wednesday, and she rarely called. "Mrs. Hayes, is something wrong?"

"I just had a feeling I should call you. My cousin Dorothy's left knee is acting up. Always happens when rain's in the air. Well, this time it's about to drive her crazy, it hurts so bad. I'm positive that hurricane is coming this way."

Jeff bit his lip to keep from laughing into the phone. "I think you're right."

"Well, you be sure and tell people to get boarded up."

"Yes, ma'am."

"Oh, and Dr. McBride, you're not going to leave that cat of yours alone in your apartment, are you? You know he just hates storms."

"No, Mrs. Hayes, I won't leave him. Thanks for calling."

Jeff shook his head as he hung up. Trust Mrs. Hayes to get her two cents in. But he did have every intention of picking up Blizzard. In fact, he'd do that as soon as he'd met the handyman at Ariel's.

Later, when he opened the door to his apartment, Blizzard looked up from his place on the couch. He jumped down and followed Jeff into the bedroom, meowing as if to ask what his owner was doing home in the middle of the afternoon.

Jeff took a overnight bag from his closet, laid it on the bed, and opened it. Immediately, Blizzard hopped inside. The cat stretched himself out and began to bathe.

"Get out, Blizzard. That's a suitcase, not a tub."

Absorbed in cleaning his paws, Blizzard paid no attention. Jeff picked up the bag and dumped him out.

"Meow!" Blizzard jumped back up on the bed. As soon as Jeff walked away, he again appropriated the suitcase.

"Damn it, cat. Get out!"

His raised voice must have impressed Blizzard because the cat climbed out of the bag and retreated to a corner of the room where he sat and glared at Jeff.

"Too bad." Jeff packed the change of clothes he'd need for broadcasting tomorrow, his shaving gear, and a few other necessities. Then he made final preparations in case the storm hit, removing breakable items from the living room and bedroom and storing them in the linen closet. He'd already taped his windows that morning.

He stood at his living room window and stared down at the Gulf. The water looked gray and rough. The tide was so high, not even an inch of beach was visible. The breeze whipped spray into the air. He thought nervously of Ariel driving to San Antonio. Thank God she was afraid of storms. That way, she wouldn't do anything reckless.

He packed a bag with cat food and litter, added Blizzard's favorite toy, a stuffed lobster, then got the cat carrier. Blizzard hissed.

"Nice boy. Come on."

The cat bared his teeth and arched his back. Jeff caught him and shoved him inside the carrier and was treated to a chorus of angry meows as they drove back to the station. He deposited the cat in Ariel's office and went to get ready for the six o'clock newscast. His face slathered with makeup, he made it to his place at the anchor desk just in time to tell viewers that the hurricane was now less than 150 miles away and posed a serious threat to the city.

Immediately after the broadcast, the phones began ringing. Some of the callers had serious concerns, like the man who asked for safety suggestions he could pass on to the nursing home where his elderly father lived. Then there were the other calls.

"Is it okay to get my hair permed before a hurricane?"

"Can you put batteries in the TV set?"

A woman called to berate Jeff for suggesting that bathtubs be filled. "I wouldn't let my dog drink water out of a tub," she huffed.

"Ma'am, that water isn't for drinking. It's for wash-ing—"

"Yes?"

"and flushing the toilet."

She gasped in horror and hung up.

AT SEVEN THAT EVENING Ariel parked in front of Chad's Spanish-style stucco house. His home was lovely, with a red-tile roof, white walls, and a wide lawn filled with shrubs and tropical flowers. Ariel wished she had a home like this, then reminded herself it was her own fault she didn't. She had chosen not to settle anywhere she'd been, always thinking of Houston as home, always seeing it as her goal. She grinned suddenly. Even if Chad won the contest, surely he wouldn't want to leave such a beau-tiful house. Maybe she'd plant that seed during their conversation tonight.

She got out of the car and lugged her suitcase up the walk, then dropped it in the doorway. Before she had a chance to ring the bell, the door opened, and she was lifted off her feet for an exuberant hug. "Hi, squirt," her brother said, setting her down. "Just in time for dinner."

"You cooked?"

"You know me better than that. Leave your suitcase right here. We'll go out for—"

They spoke in unison.

"Vegetarian."

"Chicken-fried steak."

Ariel rolled her eyes. "Chad, you can't be serious."

"Sure I am." When she glared at him, he reached in his pocket for a nickel. "I'll flip you."

"Okay. Heads, vegetarian. Tails, vegetarian."

"Watch it, kid. You're dealing with your much bigger brother," he reminded her.

"Okay, I'll give you a fair chance. Tails, chicken-fried steak."

Tails won, and they went to the crowded and noisy Black-Eyed Pea, where they sat in one of the wooden booths near the back and visited over down-home cooking and enormous glasses of ice tea.

Ariel examined her tall, blond brother critically. "You look tired, sweetie. Sure you're not working too hard? Maybe you need to slow down. You might get an ulcer."

Chad's deep blue eyes twinkled. "Sure you're not trying to sidetrack me from the contest?"

"Me?" she replied innocently.

"Yes, you. Don't worry. Only a few weeks to go and I can relax—in Houston." He regarded her over the rim of his glass. "Competition seems to agree with you. You look great."

Ariel put down her fork. "I'm in love."

"The meteorologist?"

"How'd you know?"

Chad chuckled. "Word gets around. I talked to Mother and Dad before they left for Mexico."

She sighed. "I'm crazy about him."

"And how does *he* feel?"

"We haven't talked about our feelings yet. But I'm sure we will soon. When the hurricane's over . . ."

Chad's expression turned serious. "Ariel, be careful. You haven't known him very long. Take it slow."

"Come on, Chad, don't play Big Brother with me," she said irritably, pushing her plate away. "I know what I'm doing."

He reached across the table and covered her hand with his. "I don't want to see you get hurt again."

"So says the expert on relationships."

Chad's face flushed. "A low blow. Okay, so my marriage didn't work out. I've been careful ever since."

"You've been too busy working."

He spread his hands. "Hey, let's not argue."

"Okay," she said softly.

"Good. Tell me about this guy."

"Do you have to go back to the station this evening?" When he shook his head, she beamed at him. "Great, 'cause this may take all night."

JEFF AWOKE THE NEXT morning to an ominous gray sky. Standing at the window of Ariel's office, where he and Blizzard had camped for the night, he gazed at the nearly deserted parking lot. A gust of wind caught a section of newspaper and whirled it under a car; another sent an empty plastic container skipping across the concrete. Low-hanging clouds promised rain . . . and more.

He wondered how Ariel's speech was going. With the weather holding, he didn't have to worry about her driving back. Still, he'd be glad when he had her here, safe and sound. Around eleven-thirty she'd said. He checked his watch. Only a couple of hours.

He went on the air at eight and again at nine, then came back to Ariel's office. At ten o'clock, Charles burst through the door. "Jeff, you'd better get on the air. That sucker's moving and it's headed straight for Corpus."

Jeff ran out of the room and nearly collided with the news director. "We need you on live," he puffed, handing Jeff the latest advisory. Jeff scanned the printout as he raced down the hall and into the news studio.

"This just in from the National Hurricane Center in Miami. Hurricane Ethan is now moving, heading west-northwest at twelve miles per hour. The entire Texas Gulf Coast from Brownsville to High Island—including Corpus Christi and nearby areas—is now under a hurricane warning. There is a seventy-percent probability that Ethan will strike Corpus Christi. Estimated time of landfall is four o'clock today. I repeat, we are now under a hurricane *warning*. Ethan is a potentially deadly storm with winds over 130 miles per hour. Residents should take necessary precautions *now*."

A voice in his earphone said, "Jeff, we're cutting to the mayor's office. He's making an announcement. Stay where you are. We'll come back to you immediately after."

Ariel! Jeff thought, as Mayor Cameron spoke. He had to call Ariel and tell her not to start back. "How long till I can get off the set?" he mouthed to the director.

"Five minutes."

Five minutes. It was only ten minutes past ten. Maybe the conference was running late and Ariel hadn't left San Antonio yet. He pictured her jazzy little sports car rocked back and forth by the wind and prayed he could reach her in time.

Mayor Cameron admonished residents not to panic, and the cameras cut back to the studio. Automatically, Jeff repeated instructions for orderly evacuation and precautions for those who chose to stay. Then he watched the monitor as a scene of the coastline appeared. Palm trees lined the beach, their leaves fluttering in the breeze, then suddenly swaying as a gust swept through. Behind them, swells pounded against the shore, froth whipping into the air. Jeff sat at the desk, glued to the chair by his commitment to the station, while his heart was with Ariel.

"Back to you, McBride."

"This is Jeff McBride." He repeated the latest advisory, then wound up. He jerked off his lapel mike and earphone and tore out of the studio, almost knocking over one of the technicians. In Ariel's office, he grabbed the phone. What the hell was the name of that hotel? Harder to think when you were nervous. "Marriott!" he almost shouted and began punching buttons.

There were six Marriotts in San Antonio. By the time he got the right one, his hands shook and his heart beat a tattoo in his chest. "I need to reach Ariel Foster. She was speaking at a breakfast for Women in Communications."

"I believe the breakfast was over at nine, sir," the switchboard operator told him.

"Would you page her?"

"I'll try, sir."

He waited for five interminable minutes.

"No answer," the operator said.

"Listen, this is an emergency. Can you get hold of someone from the conference and find out if Ms. Foster left San Antonio?"

"I'll send a bellman over."

He waited. Paced. Gnawed his fingernails, something he hadn't done since junior high.

At last the woman came back on the line. "Sir, the conference chairperson said Ms. Foster left as soon as her talk was finished. That was around nine, she said."

"Thank you." Nine. Too early for her to have heard the announcement about the storm. He checked his watch. Ten-thirty. She was over an hour from Corpus. He'd send her back. He dialed her car phone.

"All circuits are busy. Please try your call again."

He should have expected that. Ten thirty-two. There was time. She could make it here before the storm hit. Please, God, she had to. Taking a deep breath, he sat behind Ariel's desk and stared vacantly at the empty office.

After a while Blizzard got down from the couch, slunk across the room and curled up under the desk in a tight lump of misery. Jeff bent down to soothe the cat and get some comfort in return, but Blizzard would have none of it. He scooted farther under the desk and ignored his owner. "I should put you on television," Jeff muttered. "Blizzard the weathercat. You're the best measure of barometric pressure I know."

"Jeff—" Peg stuck her head in the door "—they're asking for you to answer some calls."

"Coming. If Ariel calls, find me." Without waiting for an answer, he sprinted down the hall.

This morning the calls were different. Serious. Scared. What part of the house would be safest? Should a swimming pool be drained? A man called saying he had no garage, only a carport. Was it safe to leave his car parked there? Between calls, Jeff tried Ariel again. He couldn't reach her.

At eleven he went back on live. The storm was closer. Now that Ethan had made a decision, he raced across the water, intent on his target—Corpus Christi.

Eleven-ten. Ariel should arrive in twenty minutes. Probably sooner. The woman drove like a maniac.

But eleven-thirty passed. The clock hands inched toward noon. And he still couldn't get through to her on the car phone. Sweat poured down Jeff's back, his gut twisted with fear and tension.

He went outside. The skies were ugly now; a dirty, menacing gray. The wind howled and caught his tie, nearly jerking it off. He went back in, strode to Peg's desk. "Any calls?"

"Nothing."

At noon he went on air again, finished at twelve-ten, and went back to Ariel's office. He should look for her, call the highway patrol. Twelve twenty-seven. Another ten minutes, and he would.

And would that do any good? She'd promised to stop if the storm came closer. She could be in any of the little towns between here and San Antonio, waiting out the storm, unable to get through to him—he hoped.

He sat down at Ariel's desk, ran his fingers over the smooth wood, picked up a letter she'd signed with her usual flourish, put it down again. He could almost smell the musky scent she wore, almost see the way she cocked her head when she listened, almost hear her laughter.

He slammed his fist on the desk. Where the hell was she? He shut his eyes and prayed.

15

ARIEL WRAPPED SWEATY hands around the steering wheel. Terror clutched at her stomach. A gust of wind slammed against the small car, grabbing the windshield wiper and almost tearing it off. Rain pelted the windows. The morning, which had started out so well, had become a waking nightmare.

She'd gotten up early, listened to the weather report, and heard with relief that the storm was still far out in the Gulf. After sharing breakfast with Chad, she dressed in a beige silk suit, repacked her overnight bag and drove downtown to give her keynote address. She'd worked hard to compose a dynamite motivational talk and, judging by the enthusiastic applause, she succeeded.

"Won't you stay for the morning session?" the conference chair invited.

Ariel shook her head. "Thanks, but I have to be back in Corpus by eleven-thirty." She checked her watch as she left the hotel. Nine o'clock. She stopped for gas, then headed for the highway. As soon as she was out of town, she flipped on the radio to KCOR Easy Listening.

The music would be interrupted for weather updates, but Ariel doubted that would be necessary. Only a few patches of cloud marred the aquamarine sky. Not a breath of wind stirred the leaves of the cottonwood trees. She smiled and hummed along with Billy Joel's "Uptown Girl."

The sky clouded as she drove east, but that didn't worry her. Rain was a fact of life along the Gulf Coast, even when hurricanes were out of season.

At ten, midway into a Bruce Springsteen number, the music abruptly stopped. "We interrupt to bring you the latest advisory on Hurricane Ethan." As she listened to the bulletin, then to the mayor's order to evacuate, Ariel's stomach dropped to her toes. The storm was racing straight toward Corpus Christi, toward her. What should she do?

"Go back to San Antonio," she muttered, then checked her odometer. Too late. She was more than halfway home. While she'd listened to the news, she'd passed the point of no return.

The sky ahead of her appeared grayer now. A puff of wind scattered a collection of dead leaves along the roadside. Just a breeze now, but it would soon become a gale.

And here she sat, alone in an automobile, miles from shelter. Yet it would take longer to return to San Antonio than to continue. If the weather got really bad, she could stop at a motel. Sure, and she'd be all alone during a raging storm in a building that might topple over. No, she wouldn't stop. She had plenty of time to get to Corpus and to the safety of Jeff's arms before four o'clock, the estimated time of landfall.

"I am calm and brave," she began in her most confident voice. "Storms do not frighten me. I will arrive in Corpus safely, long before the hurricane. I am calm and br—"

Her gaze focused on an older-model vehicle with an out-of-state license parked on the shoulder of the highway with its hood raised. A woman stood by the car door, and a small boy peered out the window. Ariel slowed as she passed, and the woman dashed forward with an arm raised, waving her hand in supplication.

Ariel braked and turned around. She couldn't ignore the woman's appeal for help, leave her out here stranded and alone. She pulled over in front of the parked vehicle and rolled her window down halfway.

The woman, her face dust-streaked, ran to the window. "Oh, thank God! I've been stuck here an hour, and no one's stopped."

"What's wrong?" Ariel asked.

"I don't know. The car started rattling and clanging, and I barely got off the road before it gave out. I—Jimmy, no!" she shrieked as the driver's-side door began to open. She ran to the car, shouting, "Don't you get out. Get back in there, right now." She slammed the door shut, then turned.

Ariel got out of her car. "Do you have a flat?"

The woman shook her head.

"Dead battery?"

"No, it turns over."

Together they peered under the hood. Ariel could change a tire, but a mechanic she was not. "Maybe we should check the oil," she suggested and leaned over to reach the dipstick. "Nope, it's fine."

"Oh, your dress."

Ariel glanced down. A spot of grease now adorned the front of her silk jacket. "No problem. It'll come out." She hoped. "Look, neither of us knows how to fix your car. Why don't I give you a ride to the nearest garage and they can send a tow truck."

"That would be wonderful." The woman stuck out a grimy hand. "I'm Susan."

Gingerly, Ariel shook her hand. "Ariel."

Susan hurried back to the car and got her son. "Let's take your suitcases, too," Ariel suggested, in case they couldn't find a mechanic and Susan had to check into a hotel in a nearby town. They lugged three heavy bags over to Ariel's car. When they were finally settled, with Susan in the front seat and the youngster and the suitcases in the space behind them, the woman said, "I can't tell you how much I appreciate your help. I was afraid I'd be out here all day, and it looks like rain."

Ariel squinted at the sky as she pulled back onto the road. Was it her imagination, or had the clouds gotten thicker in the ten minutes since she'd stopped? "You must not have been listening to the radio," she said.

"It's on the blink."

"Well, they just announced Ethan's headed this way."

"Who's Ethan?"

"A hurricane."

Susan's face paled. "Are . . . are we in danger?"

"Not yet." She couldn't believe this woman wasn't aware of the storm hovering off the coast. "Where are you from?" she asked, tempted to add, "Outer space?"

"California. My husband's stationed at the naval base in San Diego and he's on his way to Hawaii for three months, so Jimmy and I are going to stay with his folks in Corpus Christi."

"Well, you couldn't have picked a worse time," Ariel said. "The mayor's ordered an evacuation."

"I'm sure they won't leave," Susan said. "They're expecting me this morning. Right, Jimmy?" she added, turning. "We're gonna see Grammy and Pops today, huh?"

"Yep," Jimmy said, leaning forward and planting a sticky hand on Ariel's shoulder.

"That looks like a garage up ahead," Ariel said thankfully. She pulled in and parked, frowning. The place looked deserted, the doors to the bays shut. No, she saw a man inside. Susan got out and started toward the building, but the man saw her and shook his head. He opened the door and hollered, "I'm closed."

Ariel shoved her door open. "Wait a minute!" she shouted.

The man paused, then shrugged and trudged out to the car. "What do you need?" A plastic sign advertising motor oil flapped in the wind, almost drowning out his words.

"My car's stalled back on the highway," Susan said.

The fellow laughed. "I can't help you, lady. There's a storm blowing in. I'm closin' up and gettin' outta here."

"What about a tow truck?" Ariel asked.

"You can try Gallup's down the road, but I wouldn't count on them bein' open today, not with that hurricane."

"Can we use your phone?"

He scowled but agreed and gave her the number. Susan hurried inside. A few minutes later, she came back. "No one answered."

"Just what I told you."

"What am I going to do?" Susan wailed.

"Guess you'll have to leave 'er on the road. You got insurance?" the fellow asked. When she nodded, he said, "Lucky for you, cause you'd better kiss that baby goodbye. If the storm don't get 'er, buncha punks'll probably come along and strip 'er." With that dire prediction, he turned and stomped back inside the building.

Susan began to cry.

Ariel patted her shoulder. "You heard what he said. Insurance will cover the loss." Still, Susan continued sniffling as Ariel pulled back onto the highway. By now the dashboard clock read ten-fifty. "Hand me my phone, would you?" She'd better call Jeff and tell him she'd be late.

The circuits were busy. Well, what did she expect? She turned on the radio and waited for the next weather advisory.

"Ethan is moving in toward the south Texas coast at fourteen miles an hour. Present location is one hundred miles due east of Corpus Christi. Residents can expect increasingly high winds and rain, which should intensify as the hurricane approaches."

Ugly clouds, the color of dirty snow, covered the sky. The first raindrops splashed against the car windows. A gust of wind rocked the car. Susan began muttering under her breath. Ariel realized she was praying.

Ariel tried phoning the station again, as the rain became a torrent. No luck. She was certain Jeff would worry, but what could she do? Just drive. Unfortunately, though, not at her usual speed. The rain interfered with visibility, and she was forced to slow almost to a crawl.

As they neared Corpus Christi, a long line of cars passed them, headed away from the city. Rain beat a steady stream against the windshield.

"Where do your husband's folks live?" Ariel asked.

Susan stopped her incessant muttering long enough to give an address that Ariel thanked her lucky stars was only five minutes out of her way. She was twenty minutes late already. And, of course, the circuits were still busy.

It was nearly noon when they reached the city limits, fifteen minutes later instead of five when they pulled up in front of Susan's in-laws' house. As Susan raced through the downpour, Ariel noticed a note tacked to the front door. *They're gone*, she surmised, and Susan confirmed it when she plodded back to the car and climbed inside.

"They left directions to the nearest shelter." Fortunately, it was at an elementary school only a few blocks away. Ariel helped Susan with her suitcases and accepted a soggy hug and heartfelt thanks before she waded back through ankle-deep water and wearily got into her car.

The wind was higher now. As she drove along the main thoroughfare, she saw a billboard hanging precariously by one edge, shingles and other debris flying through the air, a palm tree twisting in the wind. Now that she was alone in the car, she was scared. Petrified. "I am calm and brave," she muttered. "Calm and brave— the heck with it." She was wet and miserable and more frightened than she'd been in her life.

Finally she pulled into the station parking lot. She opened the door, ready to dash inside, then realized she'd need a change of clothes. Resigned, she unlocked her trunk and lugged her overnight bag with her. "The prodigal returns," she muttered, "looking like something the cat dragged in out of the rain."

She stumbled down the hall to her office. Peg's desk was empty. She'd probably gone home. Ariel shoved her door open, stepped inside, dropped her case and leaned against the wall. Jeff sat at her desk, his head buried in his hands. "I'm back," she announced, and his head snapped up.

"Ariel!" He stared at her for an instant, then shot out of the chair. "Baby, what happened to you?" Before she could answer, he had his arms around her and was covering her face with kisses. He led her to the couch, then sat, cradling her in his lap. "I was out of my mind worrying about you. Are you okay?"

"I'm all right," she said, burrowing into his chest. "J-just wet. And c-cold."

"You're shivering. Let's get you out of these wet clothes, then you can tell me what happened." He stripped her sodden clothing off. She didn't try to help; her hands shook too badly and her teeth chattered. She huddled on the couch while he got the outfit she'd worn yesterday from her overnight bag. He helped her into the dry dress, wrapped his jacket around her and pulled her back into his lap. "Tell me," he said.

Nestling in the warmth of his embrace, she related the events of the morning. "If I'd known in time, I wouldn't have started back, but I'm glad I'm here."

"Me, too." He captured her mouth with a tender kiss, then pulled her close and stroked her back. "You must have been scared to death."

She nodded and snuggled closer against him. She wasn't a woman who craved protection, but the few times she'd needed it, Jeff had been there.

"So was I," he said. "I was ready to go out looking for you or send the Texas Rangers." His arms tightened around her. He buried his face in her hair. "Don't ever do anything like that to me again." His voice shook.

"I won't."

A knock sounded at the door. "Dr. McBride."

"Coming." He sighed. "I have to give the latest advisory. He kissed her cheek. "Rest for awhile. I'll be back."

"I can't. I have to see what's going on—"

"Steve has everything under control. Pretend you stayed in San Antonio." He wrapped his jacket around her.

Ariel's lips twitched. "You're going on in shirt-sleeves?"

"I'll risk it. Now, rest." He turned off the light. "Half an hour."

"Ten minutes." Ariel shut her eyes.

When she awoke, the room was dark. Had she slept the day away? No, this wasn't the ebony of night but a different darkness—an ugly, metallic gray-blackness, as if something sinister stood between the Earth and the Sun. Her windowpane rattled ominously as wind and rain drummed against it. She squinted at her watch. Three o'clock.

She jumped up and turned on the TV monitor, expecting a news report. Instead, she got "Our Place in the Sun."

As a grim-faced doctor approached, Elliot stood waiting. His hair was tousled, his shirttail out. The doctor put his hand on Elliot's shoulder. "I have bad news," he said. "Sabrina lost the baby."

Elliot rubbed a hand over his unshaven cheek. "Is...is she all right?"

"Physically, yes. But mentally..." The doctor sighed. "She took a severe blow to the head. When she regained consciousness, she didn't remember anything about the crash, about her life. Elliot, I'm afraid Sabrina has ... *amnesia*."

The music swelled to a melodramatic crescendo, and the screen blacked out. Ariel shook her head. The weather might be lousy in Corpus, but one could rest assured that in "Our Place in the Sun" the days were even darker.

As a commercial blared from the set, Ariel left her office and headed for Steve's. His door was ajar. She pushed it open. "Steve, I n—"

Openmouthed, she stared at the scene before her: Steve and Kara, locked in a passionate embrace. "Whoops!" she murmured, backing out the door.

Steve raised his head but didn't release Kara. "Come in."

"You sure? You two look like you don't need company."

Kara pulled a tissue from her pocket and wiped Steve's lipstick-covered face. "No, really. Besides, you can be the first to know." She beamed at Steve. "We're engaged."

"Oh, my gosh! Engaged!" Ariel rushed across the room and enveloped the two of them in a hug. "Congratulations! When's the big day?"

"We haven't gotten that far," Kara said. "Maybe Thanksgiving or Christmas."

"This calls for a celebration," Ariel said, "but I don't think this is the day for it. You'll have to take a rain check."

"Ouch." Kara giggled. "Ariel, I know you and Steve have things to discuss, so I'll get out of your way." She stood on tiptoe to kiss Steve's cheek. "See you later, honey."

Ariel took a chair and watched Steve's eyes follow Kara adoringly. "Well, once you get going, you don't waste time."

Steve's face turned the color of his hair, but he grinned at Ariel. "Nope."

"I'm glad for you," she told him. "And now, unfortunately, we have to get down to business."

They discussed coverage of the storm, then Ariel went back to her office. She stared out the window, mesmerized by the intensity of the wind. A sheet of plywood blew into the parking lot and flew into the air again. Rain swirled in torrents. An eerie purplish flash of lightning lit the sky.

"Get back!"

The harsh command made her jump. She swung around to see Jeff in her doorway, his face a mask of tension. "Has the hurricane—"

He moved toward her. "The storm's made landfall. I want you out of here—"

"No! I can't leave the station—"

"I mean, out of this room. In a place with no windows. Come on, move!" He reached under her desk, dragged a snarling Blizzard out, and dumped him in the carrier. "Go!" Jeff shouted over a crash of thunder. They ran into the hall, the cat carrier clumping against Jeff's leg. "In the newsroom!" he ordered.

Behind them glass shattered, and with a sinking heart Ariel heard the sound of rain pouring inside. "Keep going," Jeff insisted, pulling her along with him. "You can't do anything."

They rushed into the newsroom. Ariel caught her breath, then automatically pitched in to help the director. As their storm coverage intensified, she realized she welcomed the activity. After the terrifying morning in the car, it was a relief to get back to something she knew how to handle.

Stories came in from reporters in the field: a car lifted off the freeway and tossed like a toy into a parking lot below; a hospital emergency alert; a furniture store's plate-glass windows shattered; a family with five children cowering in a corner at a Red Cross shelter.

As the hours passed, as she continued to work through the noise and confusion, Ariel's gaze continually strayed to Jeff. Calm, soothing, in control, he sat at the anchor desk. His knowledge and confidence communicated itself to viewers. He was wonderful, Ariel thought. The station was lucky to have found him. *She* was lucky.

The thought suddenly occurred to her, though, that his relationship with Channel 4 was about to end. Today was the climax. After the storm was over, he'd go back to his regular job. While she . . .

If the calls from viewers were any indication, she was going to win the ratings game. Then what? Would their relationship be over? Gone with the wind? She and Jeff needed to talk.

She turned toward him. He looked tired, he sounded hoarse, but he never faltered. Her heart filled with love and pride as she watched him. He was so strong, so sure. He answered questions from viewers who called in, explaining what to expect as the storm passed over, and reported the latest developments as they came in—

The room went black.

Ariel stood, lost in the darkness, then felt someone take her by the arm. "Go sit down," Steve suggested.

"Okay, as long as we're still on the air . . ."

The emergency lights came on. Ariel found a chair and leaned back. The roar of the storm was hypnotic, lulling her into a half sleep. Day passed into night, and still she sat. And still Jeff remained on the air, giving comfort and strength to viewers and to the staff, as well. Whenever she opened her eyes, she looked toward him for reassurance.

Suddenly, the screens were blank.

"We've lost power!" someone shouted.

"Are we still broadcasting?" Ariel called.

"Yes . . . no. Damn! The tower must've gone down."

"Hell!" Steve kicked the chair in front of him. "Now what?"

"Contingency plan." Jeff made his way toward them. "As soon as the eye comes over, I'm heading for KCOR Radio." He sat down next to Ariel. "Someone let me know when it's calm. I'm going to take a break." Laying his head on her shoulder, he shut his eyes.

She wasn't sure how long they sat in the stuffy, windowless room, with the interminable howling of the storm broken only by crashes of thunder. With no air-conditioning, it was hot and sticky, almost impossible to get a breath. But at least Jeff was here.

Then, suddenly, there was no sound at all.

"The eye," someone whispered.

"Jeff!" Ariel shook him. "We have to go."

He sat up and rubbed his eyes. "Not we. *I* have to go." He raced out of the studio with Ariel at his heels.

She grabbed his arm. "I'm going with you."

He halted so abruptly she bumped into him. "Ariel, I don't have time to argue. Get back in the newsroom."

Stubbornly, she shook her head. "I won't stay here without you."

The firm set of his mouth softened. "Look, baby, I know you're afraid of storms, but—"

"I'm not afraid for myself, Jeff. I'm scared for you. I don't want you out there alone. I love you."

For a long moment, he stared at her, then he lifted a hand to her cheek. "I love you, too." Before she could say anything, he caught her hand. "Let's go. Take care of the cat," he hollered at Steve, and they ran to the door.

Outside it was eerily quiet. Not a sound, not a breeze broke the strange stillness.

They drove through deserted streets. No lights shone. Though it was nearly six in the morning, no sun broke through the steel gray sky. A stop sign stood upside down at the corner. A traffic light angled into the street. A sign on a café door that had once read Hello had lost the *o* and now read, aptly, Hell. Had she not had Jeff beside her, Ariel would have been frightened. Jeff, whom she loved and who loved her back. They'd find a way to be together.

Jeff skillfully negotiated the car, frequently swerving to avoid debris on the street. He parked in an alley beside the high-rise building where KCOR Radio was located. Without speaking, they got out. They hurried through the stillness and turned the corner.

Wind hit them full in the face.

"Run!" Jeff shouted. She tried to, but the wind thrust her back. She stumbled and fell. Glass cut into her palm; her knees scraped against the pavement. On all sides, the wind howled, flinging debris around like confetti. Rain knifed against her cheeks. She tried to get up, but couldn't. She was too terrified to move.

"Ariel!" Jeff grabbed her arm and pulled her to her feet. She staggered the last few feet to the door, he shoved it open and they lunged through. Jeff half dragged her down the hall, then stopped and pulled her against him. "Are you okay?"

"Fine," she managed.

He wiped the streaks of dirt from her face. "Stay away from doors and windows. I want you in one piece. We'll talk when this is over."

For the next six hours, with only occasional breaks, Jeff stayed on the air. Someone at the station had a pullman stove so Ariel was able to bring Jeff coffee. She would slip into the studio, set a cup down beside him, massage the tight muscles of his neck and shoulders, then slip out again. Though his voice cracked and his eyes were red-rimmed, he kept going.

Until at last someone came to tell him that the wind had died down. The hurricane was over.

Ariel's heart sang. They'd come through the storm. They loved each other. Now their future could begin.

Until at last someone came to tell him that the wind
had died down. The hurricane was over.

Ariel's heart sang. They'd come through the storm.
They loved each other. Now their lives could begin.

16

BUT THEY WEREN'T ABLE to talk about their feelings. After nearly twenty-four hours of nonstop talking, Jeff's
voice was reduced to a rasp, and he and Ariel were both
exhausted. Because the streets were flooded, they spent
the night in a hotel near the radio station.

In bed, Ariel turned to Jeff and kissed his cheek. "You
were wonderful on the air," she said drowsily. "You got
a lot of people through that storm."

He cuddled her close to him. "I'm glad I could do it."

Ariel stared into the darkness for a few minutes. "Jeff?"

"Hmm?"

"You're so good at broadcasting. You ought to continue."

"Oh, no, you don't," he croaked. "Don't think you can
sweet-talk me into something because my defenses are
down."

"Are they?"

"Not by a long shot."

Ariel sighed. "Maybe you could do a special now and
then, like Barbara Walters."

No response.

"Jeff? Jeff, are you asleep?"

A soft snore told her he was. Ariel snuggled against
him. "I've never heard you snore before," she muttered,
"but I guess snoring's okay if it only happens after hurricanes."

THE NEXT MORNING the streets were passable. As they drove back to Channel 4, Ariel stared in shock. Broken glass littered the sidewalks. Street signs twisted at crazy angles. Battered cars, broken billboards, downed trees lay strewn around them. They had to weave around branches, pieces of wood, and even metal signboards that littered the damp streets. "This is awful."

"We had more wind damage than anything," Jeff observed. "Probably in the millions."

They arrived at the station and were immediately surrounded by a crowd of staff members who all wanted to congratulate Jeff on his coverage of the hurricane.

Everyone had a story to share about the storm. Several had gone home to find their houses severely damaged. "All the living room windows blew out, and half the furniture was on the patio, all ripped to pieces." "I lost all my trees." "One of ours crashed through the dining room window." It was a storm no one would forget.

Kara came up to them. "Now that the Red Cross shelters are emptying, we need to film Debra returning to her house."

"Okay," Jeff replied. "I'll take a look at my apartment, drop off the cat, and meet the cameraman at the shelter in an hour. He turned to Ariel, his eyes meeting hers for a long, meaningful look. He lowered his voice. "See you afterward. Then we can have our talk."

"Yes." She could hardly wait.

IN THE VAN DEBRA SAT beside Jeff, chewing her fingernails. "I want to see what happened to my house, and yet I don't. Know what I mean?"

He understood exactly what she meant. He, too, was nervous.

The cameraman focused on Debra, then switched to the scene outside the window. As they came nearer the Gulf, the homes became smaller, flimsier, and the damage greater. They passed a house with a gaping hole where the roof had been. Pieces of wood lay in the yard. The front door was open. A sweaty, bare-chested man dragged a ravaged couch through it and tossed it in the yard to join a pile of broken chairs.

"Look at that," Debra moaned. She grabbed Jeff's hand and held on, her nails digging into his skin, as they turned onto her street. "I hope I don't fall apart in front of the camera."

Her house came into view and she gasped. Glass and shingles were strewn about the yard. Part of the porch sagged to the side. A large hole had been torn in the roof. "Oh, Lord. Oh, Lord," she moaned. "My house."

Jeff could think of nothing to say, nothing to do but hold her hand as the camera whirred.

The cameraman jumped out and waited for them in the yard. He began taping as soon as Debra climbed out of the van. Her eyes wide with shock and pain, she surveyed her home. "The porch," she muttered. "I was gonna paint it, put out some potted plants."

Ignoring the camera, she started up the sidewalk as though she were sleepwalking. "The living room ceiling must've fallen in. Oh, Lord, my lamp. It came from my grandma's living room." She ran up the steps, the camera following. In the doorway, she paused, then doubled over, hugging her stomach. Through a jagged hole in the ceiling, insulation and globs of wet plasterboard had rained down on the living room. An inch of brackish water covered the floor. "I can't believe this," she choked, then swiped her hand across her wet cheeks. "Oh, Lord. The shows we did were easy, but this is aw-

ful. Thousands of people are watching me fall apart on
TV."

Jeff glanced over his shoulder. "Turn off the camera."

"What?" the cameraman said.

"You heard me," Jeff ordered. "Turn it off."

"Hey, I'm supposed to be taping this."

"The hell you are. This is private." He put his arm
around Debra and led her to the couch, which had been
spared.

The cameraman cleared his throat. "Look, Dr.
McBride, I understand how you feel—how you both
feel—but I take my orders from Ms. Foster. Until she tells
me to turn off the camera, I've gotta keep going."

"Fine. We'll call her." Jeff went into the kitchen and
punched in the number of the station. He asked for Ariel,
then handed the phone to the cameraman.

"Ms. Foster, this is Dick. I'm at Debra Tucker's filming the hurricane segment, and, uh, well, Dr. McBride
would like me to stop." He listened a moment, then said,
"She's, uh, pretty upset and he'd rather not show it on
TV." He waited. "Uh-huh. Okay." He handed the receiver to Jeff and shrugged. "She said to go ahead."
Hoisting the camera to his shoulder, he left the kitchen.

"Ariel," Jeff said. "This is Debra's private pain. You
can't exploit that."

"I'm afraid we can. For one thing, it's part of the deal
we made with her. For another, it's news, and we have to
get it on the air."

Anger surged through him. "Fine, but don't expect me
to be a part of it." He slammed the phone down and went
back into the living room. Debra fumbled for a tissue and
blew her nose. "At least my grandma's lamp's okay," she
said with a shaky laugh. "We better look at the rest."

Staying out of camera range, Jeff followed her through the house. Another hole gaped in the roof above the bathroom, but fortunately, no other serious damage had occurred. "I guess I'll have to call the insurance company," Debra said shakily. "I should be getting back to the shelter now."

She shuffled back to the van. Jeff and the cameraman followed. All three sat silently on the way back. When they reached the shelter, a high school a couple of miles away, Jeff walked Debra inside. "I'm sorry about this," he said.

"Hey, it's not your fault. I appreciate what you tried to do back there." She smiled her old sassy grin. "I guess when you're a celebrity, you gotta take the bad with the good, huh? They follow Madonna around when things aren't going well for her, too."

"I'll call you tomorrow," Jeff said, "and help you clean up."

"Thanks." She hugged him and trudged down the hallway.

Jeff returned to the van. He'd have a talk with Ariel, tell her exactly what he thought of her tactics as soon as they got to the station.

But she wasn't there. "She went to check on her town house," Peg told him.

"I'll wait."

Steve passed Peg's desk, heading for his office. "Come on in," he invited and gave Jeff a broad smile. "You sure did a fantastic job yesterday and the day before."

"Thanks."

Steve tipped his chair back. "You know, when Ariel said she wanted you for those hurricane broadcasts, I wasn't sure she'd made the right choice, but that lady knows what she's doing. Yeah," he continued, "you put her over the top."

"Pardon me?"

"I mean, she's bound to win the family contest now."

"Oh, I see," Jeff said, though he didn't.

"We must've had a ninety-percent share of the audience during the hurricane. That, plus your weather reporting and, of course, the new anchorwoman, probably shot our ratings through the roof. But, hey, that's why Ariel hired you, right?"

"Right." She'd hired him to raise her ratings? What had happened to community service?

Steve smiled broadly. "So Ariel gets the prize—the Houston station—and I'll take over here. Couldn't come at a better time. You know, Kara and I are getting married."

"So I've heard. Congratulations."

"Thanks." The phone rang and Steve picked it up. After he'd said hello, he turned to Jeff. "Excuse me. I have to talk to this guy about a commercial."

"Go ahead," Jeff told him, glad for the excuse to leave, because anger was erupting like a volcano, and he didn't care to explode in front of Steve. "I'll wait in Ariel's office."

He went in, shut the door, and began to pace. He'd pieced it together from Steve's conversation: Ariel had hired him, not for altruistic reasons, but to help her win a family contest with the Houston station as the prize. He remembered the night they'd gone out with her parents, the obvious way she'd tried to impress her father, and Jeff's own feeling that he'd overlooked something about her. Now the pieces fit together, and he didn't like the finished puzzle. Not one damn bit!

"Hi."

The throaty voice behind him—the voice he'd *thought* he loved—startled him. He swung around, and she stood on tiptoe and kissed his cheek. He pulled back.

"I know you're upset about Debra. Let's talk it over."

"Yeah, let's do that—talk about Debra and a few other things." He sat across from her.

Ariel sighed. "I know it's hard to understand when you're not part of the television industry—"

"You're right. I don't understand. Don't you feel anything for Debra? Or are ratings all you think about? Exploit someone's pain, raise your ratings."

"I don't think like that at all."

"No? Explain to me how you do think."

"Jeff, Debra's story is human interest—something everyone in the city can relate to. She symbolizes what's happened to us all."

"I don't agree."

"I'm sorry, and I understand why you don't want to be involved. That's okay. We won't be able to show the piece until the tower's operational. When we do, we'll have Charles do your weather report, okay?" When he said nothing, she shifted nervously. "You said you wanted to talk about some other things."

"Yeah, contests for one. Family contests."

Her face paled. "I . . ."

"You're not going to say you don't know what I'm talking about, are you?"

"No," she answered softly.

So, what Steve had told him was true. For a moment, he'd hoped that somehow Steve had misinterpreted the situation. But clearly he hadn't. "Tell me, Ariel," he urged.

"I . . . we . . . my father put my brothers and me in competition."

"For the Houston station."

"Yes. Dad's retiring, and . . . and . . ."

"And you want to take his place. So you hired me to make it possible—"

"Yes, but not just for that." Tears pooled in her eyes.

"Damn it," he said. "You *used* me."

"Oh, Jeff, no."

"Yes. You used Debra, too. All you're interested in is your damn ratings."

"Of course, I wanted my ratings to go up. There's not a station manager in the world who doesn't want that. But I wanted to do something for the city, too." Her voice rose. "Can't you see that I could want both? Is everything in the world black-and-white to you?"

Jeff ignored her question. "Why didn't you tell me?"

"Because you wouldn't understand. You work somewhere in an ivory tower, not in the real world."

"*I* work to please myself, not my father."

She flinched as if he'd slapped her. "I . . . I don't—"

"Yes, you do, Ariel. You learned to sail to please your father. You let him pit you against your brothers in some damn fool contest."

"I didn't just want to win a contest," she insisted, her voice breaking. "Winning was a chance to work in Houston, but—"

"And you suckered me into helping you do it. I saw how you acted the night your folks were here. You showed me off like . . . like a new pet. 'See how he sits up and begs? See how he rolls over? See how he improves my audience share?' God, I thought I was in love with you." His voice shook with anger.

"Jeff." Tears rolled down her cheeks. "I love you. We have something wonderful between us. Let's not sacrifice it to . . . to television ratings."

"You've already done that." When she spread her hands, he ignored the supplicating gesture. "What we don't have anymore is trust. I told you once that was the most important thing for me." He stood. "You know, you were right. I work in an ivory tower, and I'm going back to it. I've had enough of the real world. The hurricane is over. Our agreement is over. Charles can do the weather. I'm leaving."

Without giving her a chance to respond, he strode out of her office.

17

THE NEXT DAY JEFF SPENT several hours with Debra, helping her contact her insurance company and clean some of the mess in her house. It kept him busy, kept him from thinking and, more important, from feeling.

Then, since Wayne had generously given him an entire month off, he decided to get away. Away from Corpus, away from storms, but mostly away from Ariel. He was angry and bitter. She'd hurt him in a way he'd thought impossible—deep down inside. Even his bones ached.

On Saturday he drove to Austin. Ethan's path through central Texas had skirted the state capital, causing heavy thunderstorms but no damage. When he arrived, the sun shone from a cloudless sky. He rented a cabin near Lake Travis and went fishing. It was nice to sit on the dock and drop a line in the still water. No waves, no sandy beach—nothing here to remind him of the Gulf.

Escaping from Ariel wasn't as easy. Each night he awoke wanting her. Then his body, hard with unfulfilled desire, refused to relax. He tossed fitfully, longing to hold her, to be inside her. He cursed himself for needing her. Why couldn't he put her out of his mind?

He knew his restlessness wasn't solely due to lust. His feelings for Ariel had gone far beyond that. He missed her laughter, her energy, her intelligence. Bitterness warred with longing. How could he feel this way about someone who'd deceived him?

"Damn it, go away!" he ordered the image that continued to plague him as he lounged on the porch, watching the sun-dappled lake. He needed to do something to get his mind off Ariel. Read a book. Take a hike. Neither appealed at the moment. He settled for television, sat through a local news show, then the first half of the network news.

"Residents of Corpus Christi, Texas, are still cleaning up and assessing the damage caused by Ethan, one of the decade's fiercest hurricanes."

Just what he needed. News about the storm. Jeff got up to change channels when a familiar face caught his eye. Debra! The network was showing the story of her returning home after the storm—her shock, her tears. Furious at the exploitation of his friend, Jeff had his hand on the switch when the news reporter's voice stopped him cold.

"The story of Corpus Christi resident Debra Tucker returning home after the storm brought an outpouring of aid to beleaguered survivors of the hurricane. Clothing, food, and medical supplies have been donated. Volunteers from as far away as Florida and Michigan have arrived in Corpus Christi, offering to help clean up and rebuild." As Jeff stared in shock, scenes of a man repairing Debra's roof, a nurse bandaging a small boy's leg, people spooning stew onto plates flashed by. He stared at the screen in amazement. All this from Debra's story. Her pain had touched the hearts of people all over the country.

So Ariel had been right, after all. Debra had portrayed the despair of everyone in Corpus, and people had responded.

He turned off the television, went outside, and walked down to the lake. A cool breeze touched his cheek and reminded him that summer was almost over. A summer he'd spent with Ariel. A summer that had changed his life. Did he want to go back to the way life was before? No, he answered.

He heard Ariel's voice. "Is everything in the world black-and-white to you?" She was right. She wasn't a saint; therefore, in his mind she was a sinner.

But did he want a saint? A perfect woman? Perfection, he realized, was boring. Ariel was anything but boring. He knew they were as different as two people could be. But so were Steve and Kara, and they were planning a future together. Couldn't he and Ariel do the same?

He asked himself if he could accept and forgive what she'd done. He tossed a rock into the lake, watched the ripples as it sank into the water. Like the pebble, Ariel's actions had set off reactions. No matter what her original motive, she'd achieved something for the city, for Debra—and for him. He wasn't the same man he'd been three months ago. He was more relaxed, more outgoing. And, he admitted to himself, he was in love. Still in love with Ariel.

Didn't love mean compromise, forgiveness? Or, as Ariel would say, taking the bad with the good? His unwillingness to do so, to listen to her last week, he now saw as a flaw in himself. He should have understood her desire to improve her station. Instead, he'd stalked out of her office without giving her a chance to defend herself. Abashed at the memory, he turned and started back to his cabin. He didn't want to be that kind of rigid, uncompromising man. He saw himself growing old and crotchety, alone. He didn't want that kind of life. He wanted the warmth and love that only Ariel could give.

As the sun sank and the air cooled, he realized he'd already forgiven her. Now, would she forgive him?

The next morning he packed up and drove back to Corpus Christi. He wanted to see her, straighten things out between them if he could. Damn it, he *would*. He'd do anything, even go on TV and shout it before the world: "I love you, Ariel Foster."

He arrived in Corpus in the middle of the afternoon and drove to his office. He was surprised when his co-workers greeted him as if he were a hero. He'd almost forgotten about his role in the hurricane.

Trust Moira to remind him. She appeared in his office lugging a huge cardboard carton of mail, which she proceeded to dump on his desk. "What is this?" he asked, barely able to see over the mountain of envelopes.

"Fan letters, I imagine. The *Mariner* has some, too. Check out the 'Letters to the Editor' column. Oh, and here are the papers from the last few days. You made the front page on Sunday."

Dumbfounded, Jeff stared at his picture beneath a headline proclaiming: From Hunk To Hero. Weatherman Calms Citizens' Fears During Storm.

Meteorologist Dr. Jeff McBride was already a familiar sight to residents of Corpus Christi before Hurricane Ethan made his name a household word. During the summer he provided weekly hurricane safety tips on Channel 4 and became known as the Hurricane Hunk. But when Ethan struck the city last week, the Oklahoma-born Ph.D. went from Hurricane Hunk to Hurricane Hero. Broadcasting for nearly twenty-four hours straight, first on TV and then on KCOR Radio when Channel 4's transmitter went out, McBride talked frightened Corpus

Christians through the storm. His calm, authoritative manner and his knowledge of hurricanes made his the voice to listen to, and thousands of residents tuned in as Ethan raged through the city. Letters of appreciation for McBride's coverage have poured in to City Hall and to the *Mariner*. At least one area civic club is petitioning the mayor to name a street in McBride's honor. Mayor Cameron said he was open to the possibility and would bring it before the city council.

"And here are your phone messages," Moira said when he put the paper down. She picked up the top one and cleared her throat. "This one's from one of the networks. They're interested in doing a movie-of-the-week about you."

"A movie? That's . . . that's ridiculous."

"I agree. With your moon in Jupiter, the stars aren't favorable for that kind of thing. On the other hand, if David Letterman wants you for his show, go for it."

Jeff burst out laughing. "Does one of your little books say, 'Take Letterman'?"

"Not in so many words. You have to know how to interpret the messages." When Jeff leaned back and roared with glee, she put her nose in the air. "Don't be so quick to dismiss astrology. Everything I've told you has come true."

He couldn't argue with that. "What's my forecast for tomorrow?"

Moira pursed her lips. "You'll have to find that out tomorrow." She flounced out of the room.

Jeff glanced at some of the letters, then put them back in the box. Reading them all would take days. He left his office and went to catch Wayne before he left for the day.

"I'm glad you're back early, Jeff," his boss said. "There's a hitch in the South Texas Marine Services project, and we need to talk. Let's meet tomorrow around ten-thirty."

"Sure." Jeff knew from experience that the meeting would last all day. He decided he'd wait to see Ariel until tomorrow night. There was something he needed to do first.

Back in his office, he typed out a letter, then called the news editor of the *Mariner* to tell him he'd be sending a fax. He checked the letter once more.

I am flattered by your article calling me the Hurricane Hero, but the credit belongs not to me, but to Ariel Foster, manager of Channel 4. The idea of broadcasting a series on hurricane safety was entirely hers. I was just the person in front of the camera. If anyone deserves to be called a hero or heroine, the honor belongs to Ariel Foster and her dedicated staff.

Before they talked, he wanted Ariel to see the letter, which the editor assured him would be printed tomorrow on the front page.

ARIEL FELT A SENSE OF déjà vu as she parked in front of Jeff's office early the next morning. Not so long ago, she'd come here for the first time, but so much had happened since. So much good, and then the sorry end. But the letter on the front page of the *Mariner* this morning had made her take heart. Surely it meant something; surely it was a message to her, offering a truce of sorts. Only she wanted more than a truce; she wanted a reconciliation. She wanted Jeff.

She checked her makeup in the visor mirror, straightened her raspberry linen skirt and blouse, squared her shoulders and strode into the building. The last time she'd been here, she'd viewed the visit as a challenge. This time was so much more important. Television ratings had been at stake before. Now the rest of her life hung in the balance. She'd thought she'd been in love once before. What she'd felt had been a pale imitation of the real thing. But why did love have to hurt?

She'd spent the week Jeff was gone crying into her pillow, soul-searching, admitting some hard truths about herself. She only hoped he'd listen when she told him what she'd learned.

She pushed open the door of Gulf Coast Weather Technology and found Jeff's secretary seated at her desk, highlighting something in the morning paper.

Moira looked up and smiled. "Ms. Foster, how nice to see you. Is Jeff expecting you?"

Ariel gave her a breezy smile. No one watching her would guess her heart was pounding and the hand clasping her purse was damp with sweat. "No, I'm pretending to have an appointment."

Moira nodded, her eyes twinkling. "Like the last time. Come on, and I'll announce you." She glided across the waiting room and knocked briskly on Jeff's door, opened it, then slipped away. Ariel stood in the doorway, unable to move.

Jeff turned and stared. His face showed both surprise and wariness. "Ariel," he murmured. "You're here again without an appointment."

Ariel's hands trembled, her breath caught in her throat. More than anything, she wanted to fling herself into Jeff's arms. But she stood in the doorway and pasted a smile on her face. "If at first you succeed, try the same plan again," she said, as if she had all the confidence in the world.

"Sit down," Jeff said. His expression and his voice told her nothing of his feelings.

She took the chair across from him and sat silently. Her brain had turned to mush. Every word she'd rehearsed deserted her.

"Why did you come?" Jeff asked softly, his smoky gray eyes boring into hers.

"I wanted to talk to you."

"About what?"

"Debra." That was easiest. "Have you spoken to her?"

"No, I've been out of town, but I saw her on the network news."

"And?" She could only hope he'd been pleased.

"You were right. She touched people's hearts, and they responded."

Ariel nodded. "Yes, she made them care. And the best part is that a man she met at the Red Cross shelter saw the story when we first ran it and offered to fix her roof. I think he's interested in more than roofing. He took her out for dinner Tuesday, and they're going dancing this weekend."

"I'm glad something positive came out of the storm."

"Yes," Ariel agreed, then smiled. "I guess it's an ill wind that blows no good."

"One of your proverbs that's true," Jeff said but didn't smile back.

She paused for a moment, gathering courage for what she had to say next. "I saw your letter in this morning's *Mariner*. Thank you for giving me credit, but you're the one who did the work. You deserve to be called a hero."

"I suppose I'd rather be called a hero than a hunk."

He was both—and much more, in her eyes. She took a breath. "You were right about a lot of things, Jeff. I'd like to talk about what happened between us."

"So would I."

She raised her eyes to his, but still could read nothing in his dark gaze. She'd just have to blurt out everything and pray. "When I asked you to do the hurricane segments, my first thought was for myself. I hired you first and foremost to help my station." She stared at the hands clenched in her lap. "But as time went on, what we— what *you*—provided for the community became just as important to me. Then more important. I don't know if you can believe that, but it's true."

"I believe you."

She let out a breath. Now for the hardest part. "I did a lot of thinking after you walked out of my office. It wasn't easy to admit to myself, but you were right. About so many things. My father—"

"Ariel . . ." His voice was gentle, and for the first time, she saw something in his eyes, something that gave her hope.

"Let me finish. I . . . I never realized how much I wanted to please him. Not just to outdo Chad and Daniel, but to shine for him. That's one reason I wanted to win the contest. That was foolish of me. I thought a lot this week and realized I didn't need a contest to earn my father's love and attention. I had them all along." She took a shaky breath. "There's another reason I wanted to win. Since I was a teenager and went off to prep school, I've been a vagabond. All I've ever done is move. First to one city, then another. I haven't had a real home in years. I wanted some permanence in my life. I wanted to get back to Houston. I was . . . desperate."

"I think I do understand." He reached across the desk to cover her hand with his.

Oh, God, to touch him again. Did he feel it, too—this bond they'd forged?

"I understand some things about myself, too," Jeff said. "I was too quick to judge. Instead of listening, I condemned you without a trial. I'm sorry."

Tears welled in her eyes. "It's okay."

"Is your ratings contest over?" he asked.

"Yes."

"Who won?"

"I did."

"I guess you'll be moving to Houston, then." His voice flat, he removed his hand from hers.

That hurt as surely as if he'd struck her. He was still angry, or maybe he didn't care. She'd thought, she'd hoped...but apparently she'd been wrong. She'd tell him the rest, then leave. If she choked on every word, she'd get through the next two minutes without a tear. "No," she said. "By the time I found out I'd won, the contest didn't mean anything to me. I've decided to stay in Corpus. Channel 4 is number one now, and I have some ideas that will keep it there. Chad will go to Houston, and Steve will take his place at the San Antonio station. I've realized I want the permanence here."

"You're staying?"

"Yes. I even bought some things for the house. Patio furniture. I know it doesn't sound like much, but it's important to me." She gave him a shaky smile. "Home isn't a city. It's where the heart is." *And my heart belongs to you*, she added silently. She stood and forced a light tone. "Besides, I'd rather be a big fish in a little pond than get lost in a huge pond like Houston."

"Is there room in your pond for another fish?"

"Wh-what do you mean?"

He rose, walked around his desk, took her hands in his and drew her gently toward him. "I'd rather be a husband than a hunk *or* a hero. If you'd consider being a wife, we could share that pond."

For a moment, she stood motionless. Everything she'd dreamed of, everything she'd longed for was here before her. She threw her arms around his neck. "Yes. Oh, yes!"

How glorious to taste his lips again, to feel his heart pounding against her own, and to know that he was hers! She drew back and looked up at him. "Winning isn't everything. Loving you is."

"For me, too."

Ariel sighed and kissed him. "All's well that ends well."

"Huh-uh. For once, my love, you picked the wrong platitude. This isn't the end. It's the beginning."

Then he kissed her again. And again.

This month's
irresistible novels from

Temptation

IN PRAISE OF YOUNGER MEN by Lyn Ellis

Will Case was too big, far too attractive and much, much too sexy. And for the next few months, he would be sharing a cabin with Carolina. Will was also best friends with her little brother—and the same age!

THE RELUCTANT HUNK by Lorna Michaels

Ariel Foster wanted Jeff McBride to do a series for her TV station. She knew every woman in town would tune in to watch the drop-dead gorgeous man, if only she could persuade him to work for her. But she soon realised she wanted the reluctant hunk for herself.

BACHELOR HUSBAND by Kate Hoffmann

Come live and love in L.A. with the tenants of Bachelors Arms. The first in a captivating new mini-series.

Tru Hallihan lives in this trendy apartment block and has no thoughts of settling down. But he can't resist a bet to date popular radio presenter, Caroline Leighton. Caroline will only co-operate at a price—Tru must pose as her husband for a day!

SECOND-HAND BRIDE by Roseanne Williams

Brynn had married Flint Wilder knowing he was on the rebound from her twin sister, Laurel. Six months later, Brynn had left Flint, fearing she'd never be more than a substitute for her twin. Now Brynn was back in town and Flint seemed hell-bent on making up. But could she ever be sure she wasn't just a stand-in for her sister?

Spoil yourself next month
with these four novels from

THE TWELVE GIFTS OF CHRISTMAS
by Rita Clay Estrada

Pete Cade might be the hunk every woman dreams of finding
under her tree, but he wasn't ready to give the special gift at
the top of Carly Michaels's Christmas list—a father for her
daughter.

THE STRONG SILENT TYPE by Kate Hoffmann

*Come live and love in L.A. with the tenants of Bachelors Arms.
Second in a captivating mini-series.*

Strong and silent Josh Banks had never been the subject of
gossip before. But suddenly everyone was warning him about
wild women—ever since he'd promised to keep party girl
Taryn Wilde out of trouble. He could handle her…couldn't he?

FANCY-FREE by Carrie Alexander

Some residents don't approve of newcomer Fancy O'Brien
taking a bath—in town—to publicize the opening of her bath
boutique. But Jeremiah Quick is glad Fancy has arrived. He
thinks Fancy's the right woman for him. Too bad *Fancy* thinks
he's the right man for her mother…

BARGAIN BASEMENT BABY by Leandra Logan

Marriage had never appealed to Greg Baron. But since he was
going to be a father, he didn't have much choice. If only the
Baron family wasn't so thrilled to finally have an heir. If only
his image of Jane Haley pregnant wasn't so delectable…